The Carrier

Diana Ryan

CreateSpace ISBN-13: 978-1511917964
CreateSpace ISBN-10:1511917962

To my wonderful parents who instilled in me the virtues of hard work, pursuing your dreams, and believing in yourself.

Prologue

Arthur Gardner sat with his newlywed wife at the round kitchen table in their modest cabin. She was pregnant with their first child and was beginning to show a baby bump under her light blue kitchen apron. A large man in every extent of the word, Arthur spent his days tending cattle and growing corn on his thirty acres, but also caring deeply for his wife.

"Pass the corn please, Edna, dear." Arthur reached out for the bowl, but just as Edna was about to pass it, a strange sound rang out and a loud boom shook the house. Edna dropped the bowl of corn and the china smashed on the wooden table.

"What in the Sam Hill was that?" Arthur craned his neck to look out the kitchen window, his eyes widening when he saw a bright blue glow coming from the cornfield.

"Holy Mary. The sky is falling," Edna whispered under her breath as she quickly made the sign of the cross.

Arthur sprang up, grabbed the rifle from the nail by the door, and instructed his wife to take cover under the stairs. Edna rushed over to the tiny space, squeezing herself in. He dashed out the back door and walked briskly toward the glow in the field. It couldn't be fire—he didn't see any smoke, and besides, the glimmer was blue.

Arthur pulled his gun up to his shoulder, cocked it, and cautiously approached the curious light. But when he got close enough to really see the source, he let his rifle fall to the ground and knelt down in the field. A large divot had been scooped out of the dirt, and inside the soil bowl was a luminous blue rock. It wasn't on fire. It was simply glowing, and although it was odd, it seemed to be no threat to Arthur or his wife.

The blue rock was the size of a small cat coiled up. Curiously, Arthur looked up and saw nothing but a dark black sky and a few shining stars scattered about. He walked to the barn and returned to the object with a brown woolen blanket. Arthur thoughtfully covered the rock and then returned inside to tend to his wife.

Arthur slept little that night and dreamt of strange beings descending from the sky. In the morning he went out to the site of the glowing blue rock and carefully lifted the blanket to peek underneath. The rock was still sitting safely in its dirt nest, but the rock's light had diminished considerably and now simply looked like a shiny, very smooth blue gem. Arthur put on his barn gloves and picked up the rock. As he turned it in his hand, he decided it was extraordinarily beautiful and Arthur was sure it must be very valuable.

Edna was waiting quietly at the kitchen table for her husband to return from the field. She was immediately enthralled by the blue orb and insisted that Arthur build a glass box to display the object on the pie safe in the dining room.

There it sat for many years until it was passed down through the generations of the Gardner family. It became an object of wonder to some, and a possession of value to others, but everyone who handled it knew it contained the mysteries of faraway places.

Chapter One

The sound of my amplified voice bounced off tall stone walls and echoed down the swift river channel. I stood on the roof platform of the tour boat, facing a crowd of forty people, many of whom were not paying any attention to me.

"The Kilbourn Dam was a source of controversy when it was built in 1908," I announced. "Henry Hamilton Bennett, known for his innovative photography of Wisconsin Dells, knew that constructing the dam on the Wisconsin River would raise the water level twenty feet. This would drastically cover much of the gorgeous, rocky scenery, and it would be forever lost to the deep, dark, swirling waters."

As the tour boat turned with the bend in the river, my cheek felt the soft light of the sun rising over the pine trees to the east.

The first tour of the day was always my favorite. Nature was waking up all around me, and there were usually only the most pleasant of tourists on my tour boat: elderly couples, nature hippies, and inquisitive, middle-aged people with very well behaved children. These were the kind of tourists that wore fanny packs and took detailed notes on little yellow legal pads throughout the tour.

As the day went on, the quality of tourists usually took a considerable and steep dive, right up to the last boat of the day (lovingly called "The Owl" by boat employees), which was populated with obnoxious, out-of-control children, tourists who didn't speak a lick of English, and families who had spent the entire day at Noah's Ark Waterpark and were crabby, tired, and burnt to a crisp. None of the people from this dysfunctional group seemed to listen to a word I said.

"H.H. Bennett opposed the building of the power dam and he fought his battle until 1908 when he died. The dam was completed in 1909, and just as Bennett predicted, miles upon miles of the most beautiful rock formations you've ever seen were flooded and still remain underwater today."

Wisconsin Dells, located forty-five minutes north of the capital of Wisconsin, has been a tourist town for more than one hundred and fifty years. With an off-season population of just over seven thousand people, every summer the town comes to life with visitors, brimming the tiny city's capacity to almost ten times that in three months.

Tour guides were one of the most sought-after summer jobs by the local kids because in a few months you could easily make enough dough to pay tuition at a state college and didn't have to work your butt off doing it. The Dells Boat Tours hired fifteen or so female tour guides and just as many male drivers each summer. They were paired up in teams to work as a crew upon a boat assigned to them for three months.

Sometimes that got pretty interesting. My first driver, Justin, was amazingly hot and had just turned twenty-one. I was fifteen. We had nothing in common, so I spent most of the summer staring at his perfectly curved ass while he drove the boat in silence.

Actually, it wasn't interesting at all.

Now I worked with Jack, who was once my middle school health teacher. A bit weird, perhaps, but since I became a college student, we got along comfortably, and I truly enjoyed working as a team with him.

Jack, a guy of average height and slightly overweight build, had buttery-blonde hair cut short and a kind, round face. He was in his mid-thirties and recently divorced, and although he didn't talk too much about it, I could tell he was genuinely hurt from whatever had happened. His bright green eyes always seemed so lonely. I tried to be a good friend to him and, thankfully, our difference in age didn't seem to stand in the way too much. Luckily he could carry on a conversation, because his ass wasn't something to stare at.

I climbed down the ladder built into the front of the *General Bailey*, our trusty tour boat. The *Bailey* was one out of four in a fleet of very large and very blue tour boats housed at the docks on the Lower Dells of the Wisconsin River. To Jack and me, the *Bailey* was our favorite, although we never could quite put our finger on why.

I paused for a second, standing on the bow of the boat to take in a few lungfuls of the warm summer breeze and to gaze at the inexplicably beautiful scenery that surrounded me. I happily exhaled—five summers and I still couldn't get enough.

I left the bow and took the next four broad stairs into the lower level of the boat. Jack had placed a bendable pirate figure on my chair and had formed its hands and legs into a pose only Michael Jackson would make.

"Nice," I said, and moved the pirate to a place of honor on the dash above the dials and steering wheel. I turned to the black iPod on the counter and switched on the background music for my next song. I sang out "Following the River," a gentle ballad written specifically for the boat tours. My voice filled the empty shorelines and bounced off the rocky walls.

I used to be a non-singing Upper Dells guide for a few years until my boss, Darren, came to see his family friend perform in the Dells High School spring musical, and guess who was also singing her heart out? He came up to me after the curtain closed and offered me a job as a singing tour guide on the Lower Dells for the next summer.

My pretty song ended and I switched off the iPod as the tourists applauded their gratitude for me. I continued with my tour commentary: "One hundred years ago people flocked by the trainful to take a spectacular two-decked, paddle wheel tour boat upriver and view scenery more beautiful than anything from their wildest dreams."

Out of the corner of my eye I could see Jack using the bendable pirate to try to make me laugh. It was clinging for life to the spokes of the steering wheel, dancing around the dashboard, and then hiding behind the throttles. It was Jack's mission each day to try to make me laugh so hard that I couldn't continue with my tour. So far, he had not succeeded.

Continuing with my commentary, I pointed out the window with the classic two-finger tour guide point. "Tens of thousands of years ago, glacial meltwater swiftly charged through this area, creating the river channel and carving some really interesting rock formations." One of the kids in the front row gave an awfully loud yawn. Not typical for the coveted first-tour passenger group. His mother nudged him in the ribs with her elbow.

Jack decided to wake that kid up and get some wind blowing through his hair, so he shoved the throttles forward and cruised through the brown river channel into the Rocky Island Region—a part of the river where sandstone islands, literally the size of houses, were sporadically deposited in the channel by Mother Nature herself. Pilots were trained to maneuver the boats between the islands to impress the tourists by traveling within inches of the huge rock islands.

Once last season Jack had been still hungover from a night at the bar, and I had feared a scene from *Titanic* might be in our near future. I held my eyes closed tight as we made it through the channel, just barely, and then Jack turned to me and said, "I think I'm still drunk." Grumpy and not impressed, I was able to steer the boat back to the docks, and then I forced him to down a large cup of coffee and nap it off on the back deck of the *Bailey* between trips.

I glanced behind me and saw that the bendable pirate was now doing the splits on Jack's head. I wondered what the tourists on the bottom deck were thinking about their comedic captain. One look around, however, revealed that the passengers inhabiting the chairs on the bottom deck were all busy in their own worlds: a middle-aged couple looking out the window, teenagers staring into each other's eyes, and a young couple trying to calm a crying baby.

I went on with my tour while observing my distracted audience. "Native Americans who lived in this area many years ago played a part in naming the river. They called the river '*Meskousing*,' which translates roughly into 'river of rock.' Over time, the name transformed into the French word, '*Ouisconsin*,' most likely influenced by French traders and explorers. These explorers also coined the term '*Dalles*,' which means flat layers of rock. The two words appropriately merged together to eventually form the American spelling of Wisconsin Dells."

Thirty minutes later we arrived back at the huge blue metal dock, and I jumped the four-foot gap like a riverboat ninja with the stern line in my hands. I pulled the back end of the boat with all my might until it matched up with the cleat on the dock. This looks more impressive than it really is, and I usually make a big show of pulling in the boat, especially if there are passengers sitting on the stern bench watching my every move. I quickly whipped out my half-loop knot over the cleat, and Jack switched off the engine. "All ashore who's going ashore!" I yelled at the tourists—they loved hearing all that boat lingo. These, the loveliest of passengers, stepped off one at a time, some handing me tips, and almost all giving me compliments on my singing.

Once all the passengers had disembarked, Jack and I hung out on the back deck. It was one of the first days we'd worked together this summer, so we spent most of the time chatting about the last school year. I had recently finished up my first year studying to be a teacher at the University of Wisconsin–Stevens Point and had many stories to share of my first college experience. The truth was that last year was a little rough academically, but I wasn't ready to get into all that quite yet. It would come out in time, I was sure. Jack listened and said a little about his past year teaching health to hormonal middle schoolers.

Soon enough, our break was over, and it was time for our next tour. Crews on the Lower Dells give an average of seven tours a day, and we had only knocked out one so far. I prepared to load up our next group of passengers when I spied Darren walking down the dock several hundred feet away with someone by his side. His mysterious guest also wore the boat uniform—navy blue cargo shorts and a white short-sleeved button-down shirt with epaulets on the shoulders. It was not the best apparel for a summer tan. My co-worker Rachel, who had the body of a Hawaiian Tropic's model, would regularly wear a bright orange bikini under her boat uniform and strip down to her swim wear, lounge out of the back deck of her tour boat, and catch some rays between trips. We all knew why she made more money in tips than the rest of us, but we didn't dare use her skin-baring technique.

As they got closer, I noticed that the young man walking next to Darren looked about my age, and the minute I looked at his face, I felt my chest constrict, like someone was squeezing my lungs with their bare hands. I took a sharp intake of breath and stared at the dock, trying to pull myself together, but I was well aware that the guy was getting closer.

I dared to look up again. Most of his face had soft, handsome features, but his nose had an adorable sharp edge to it. Gelled, dark hair with trendy sideburns capped off his slim, average-height figure. He had a cute, broad smile on his face, complete with dreamy dimples, and he was staring right at me. I tried to look away but couldn't peel my eyes off the spot where he was walking. He was one of the most gorgeous men I had ever seen.

Darren finally approached the end of the dock where Jack and I were loading our passengers. "Good morning, Ava, Jack. We've hired a new ticket agent, Nolan Hill, and I want him to ride along with you for a trip. You've gotta know the product you're selling, right?" Darren barked out a laugh that only a big burly boss would give. Jack gave a laugh, too, which I was sure was purely politeness.

Wait! This handsome guy is riding along with us this trip?

Suddenly the job that I had had no problem performing a million times before seemed impossible to complete. I panicked inside as those hands on my lungs squeezed tighter. I couldn't find a word to reply to my boss or his guest. Jack caught my eye, spied my terror, and, like a good friend, jumped in to cover for me.

Jack stuck out his hand to give a hearty handshake. "Hey, Nolan. Welcome to DBT, and aboard the *General Bailey*. You can sit up front with us. Follow me." He turned off the dock, entered the back deck, and then descended the stairs to the bottom area.

Nolan's delightful face lit up and he said, "Hi, Ava. It's really nice to meet you." He paused and smiled a bright, flirty smile, and then leaned in closer so that only I could hear his quiet voice. He raised his eyebrows somewhat suggestively. "Are you really going to sing? Darren told me there are singing tour guides on the Lower Dells."

I opened my mouth to acknowledge him, but nothing came out, so he smiled one more time and then turned and followed the same path Jack took.

I let out the breath I had been holding. What did he just do to me?

Come back! I'll coax some words out somehow!

But he didn't hear my thoughts, of course, and I saw him take a seat in the front row.

Right up front!

My heart raced as I felt my mouth drying out. How would I be able to sing on this tour?

Darren wished me a great tour and then walked down the dock and up the stairs to talk to the dispatcher, Rob, at street level. I loaded the rest of the passengers, and when I got the "okay" wave from Rob, I untied the bow and stern, closed the gate on the back deck with shaking hands, and cautiously walked down the four steps to the bottom deck of the boat. There were two families seated by the windows, but it was mostly empty.

Nolan sat alone in the very first row of chairs. I walked up the aisle right past him and took my seat on my high stool upfront. Nolan eagerly looked up at Jack and me, and I thought the butterflies in my stomach were going to fly up my esophagus and spew out of my mouth. What would Jack do if I threw up right there at his feet as he was welcoming the passengers onto our boat?

"At this point I'm going to turn the microphone over to your talented and very single—I mean lovely—tour guide, Ava." Jack handed the microphone over to me with a not-at-all subtle wink, and I switched on the iPod, scowling at him. A cartoony sounding boat whistle rang out and "Welcome to the Riverboat" began.

I had figured out early on that in order to be a successful singing tour guide you had to wholeheartedly embrace the cheesiness of "Welcome to the Riverboat," which was an overly peppy tune that sounded like a kid's song, lyrics that obnoxiously rhymed, and one part that requires the guide to ask a passenger his or her name and sing it. If you weren't confident enough to ham it up, you'd be overcome with embarrassment and the whole thing would be a disaster.

I found some courage deep inside of me, calmed a few of those butterflies in my gut, and belted out a great rendition of "Welcome to the Riverboat." I took the stairs to the upper deck only a few lines into the song, not wanting to stay on the bottom and risk another look from Nolan.

I returned to the bottom deck part way through the tour, when I felt my nervousness had subsided a little. It was clear to me that this was Nolan's first trip through the Dells. He was constantly looking out the window and seemed very interested in all the history and geology I was sharing. As I continued the tour, I felt more and more comfortable, and I was able to give one of the best tours of my life.

On the way back upstream, I granted the tourists some time without commentary to sit back and enjoy the scenery. Some imaginary voice inside me told me to go sit next to Nolan in the front row. Somehow, as soon as I sat down, I felt an odd sense of calm wash over me.

"You're a lucky lady," he said. "I mean, because you get to spend all day out here. I haven't seen anything this beautiful before." He was staring out the window at the hundred-foot rock cliffs surrounding him. "In Deforest, all we have are corn fields." Without looking back from the window he asked, "Are you from the area?"

"Yeah, my family and I have lived in the Dells all my life. Actually, my dad's ancestors moved here from England more than a hundred years ago and his family has lived here ever since. Tourists don't believe that people actually live in the Dells, but just beyond the main drag you'll find a community of happy Midwestern folk simply living their lives and trying to ignore the craziness a few blocks over. Every summer season, when the tourists really began to arrive and we hear the police sirens, helicopter tours, and carnival ride noises, my mother would say, 'The crazies are in town!' "

I continued my story, even though he hadn't indicated he was actually interested in listening to me. "My sister and I spent most of our summers pretending we were fish at the community pool, racing our bikes around the block, or playing with the neighbor girls in our large backyard. We were basically oblivious to the fifty thousand tourists that inhabited our little town between Memorial Day and Labor Day. Every now and then, however, my family used to play tourist. We'd put on our fanny packs and walk downtown to check out what was new in the stores and attractions on Broadway. It was a strange childhood, but I wouldn't change it for anything."

I stopped for a comment from Nolan, but he said nothing and continued to stare at the scenery. Was he ignoring me? My opinion of the company's newest ticket agent just went downhill. Maybe this guy was a complete jerk. I went on anyway.

"When I was fourteen I got a job working for the Boat Tours. On the Upper Dells tour, the boat stops and you take a walking tour through a rocky canyon called Witches Gulch, see a trained dog jump across a chasm at Stand Rock, and then make an optional stop at Cold Water Canyon. I was a walking tour guide at the Canyon and had a blast wasting my summer days away with a few other fourteen-year-olds. A couple of years later, at sixteen, the Canyon closed and I became one of the youngest boat guides to work for DBT. I've spent every summer of the past four years educating and entertaining thousands of tourists on my tour boats."

I continued mostly for myself now, as I was sure he was tuning me out, still staring out the window. "You know, I've fallen in love with the Dells and the Wisconsin River. I think I've been up and down this river over two thousand times, and every time I come back I see something new. It's so quiet and peaceful at times, and at others it's full of speedboats and jet skis and seems so exciting! It never gets old to me. I think that's why I love my job. Best summer job ever."

I was looking down at the high school class ring on my finger now, turning it with my other hand. Memories of a popular girl who made the honor roll and dated the quarterback filled my head. Why hadn't college been what I expected? Lost in my thoughts, I forgot for a second that Nolan was right next to me, but when I looked up, he was still staring out the window.

I just poured my heart out! Did he even hear a word I said? I let out a frustrated sigh, hoping it was loud enough for Nolan to catch my hint.

But he said nothing for what seemed like a few minutes. It was a very awkward silence, and I couldn't think of anything else to say to fill the blank space between us. Right when I was about to get up, disappointed, and join Jack at the wheel, I heard Nolan exhale loudly.

"Now I know I've made the right decision." He finally turned from the window and I swear I saw something emotional behind his eyes. "I had quite a time trying to decide if I should leave home and take this job. But now I know I'm right where I'm supposed to be."

Perhaps I was all wrong about this guy.

"Welcome to the Dells, Nolan. Before long, you'll be in love." I turned to look out the window and smiled. I had the most incredible feeling of hope in my heart.

Chapter Two

Almost a week later I was heading downriver on my second to last tour of the day. I absent-mindedly stared down into the swirling, brown water past the deck below my feet, but suddenly my sight went fuzzy. The water seemed to pixelate into big, brown, blurry squares. It really was a strange sight. I blinked rapidly and rubbed my eyes until the peculiar view faded away.

What was that about?

A yawn escaped my throat. Perhaps I needed to get more sleep.

I slowly dared to look back down at the water. It looked normal and perfectly brown again. I hadn't had any water for a while; maybe I was dehydrated.

Funny how something so basic and natural as a river seemed so precious and beautiful to me when tens of thousands of people took it for granted each day. Instead of discovering a spectacular natural world full of rich history and Native American legend, most visitors to the Dells were working on their tans at the waterparks or putting the pedal to the metal around the go-kart tracks. Tourism for the boats had been on a severe downhill trend for the last few decades, and it didn't make much sense to me.

The golden summer sun was setting quietly beneath the breathtaking rocky cliffs on the shoreline. Gently, warm breezes blew through my brown hair as I stood gripping the microphone in my hands. I waited for Jack to expertly swing the boat around so the tourists could get the perfect vantage point of Hawk's Beak.

"Our next point of interest was once featured on the cover of *Time Magazine*. To find Hawk's Beak, follow the shoreline..." I spoke empty words as my mind drifted off. It was like I was on autopilot. I could speak the sentences of my tour while thinking of something else. I hadn't been back on the job too long yet this summer, but years ago, my boat tour had been ingrained in my mind like a rubber stamp. It was sheer talent that, four years later, I could still give tours like the info was all fresh and new. Then again, it was only early June, and the monotony of the job tended to wear on guides by mid-August. Besides all of that, my mind seemed to be off on tangents these days.

Near the end of the tour, I stood in the tiny back closet, quickly calculating the number of guidebooks I had just sold.

God, it's suffocating in here.

The tiny hole in the wall did not let in nearly enough air to dry the sweat beading up on my bra line.

In order to insure that tour guides gave their very best tour each and every time they took a trip downriver, the boat company decided to pay their employees with commission from the sales of a guidebook. This guidebook was fifteen pages of scenes from the Dells as well as old, sepia-toned photos taken by H.H. Bennett more than a hundred years before. There were pictures of Ho-Chunk leaders in full garb, lumbermen attempting to ride their log rafts through the rapids of the narrows, and photos of present-day tour boats. On the end of each page were copies of the photos in postcard form, perfect for sending back to loved ones.

This seemed to be a good system for the guides, as long as they had boats filled with passengers. Early in the season, on a rainy day with only a few passengers to count on each boat, a guide could feasibly walk away making only thirty dollars for an eight-hour shift. Then again, in the middle of July when tourism was at its peak in the Dells, a guide could easily rake in a hundred dollars or more a day.

A quick subtraction and then multiplication problem in my head forced me to count the money in my hands.

Sweet, they matched.

I took out a small hunk of cash from my bulky cargo shorts, folded in the new money, and then shoved the whole thing back in my pocket.

I pushed open the door, breathing in the cool, fresh river air, and made my way back up the aisle to the front to sit next to Captain Jack, who was enjoying the wind flowing swiftly through the front hatch.

"How'd we do?" Jack questioned me.

"We're thirty-nine for five," I said. Out of the corner of my eye, I noticed a grimace on Jack's face as I leaned over to grab my yellow mini-notebook off the front counter. I noted the day's numbers and then assured him, "But it's only June 9th."

Jack sighed under his breath. "Yeah, I guess you're right."

Selling thirty-nine souvenir picture books in five trips was less than stellar by anyone's standards—even for early June. We sat through the rest of the ride upriver in silence.

My mind was not a bit quiet, though. It was filled with questions about dreamy Nolan. It had been five days since I met him on my boat that morning and I hadn't seen him since. I figured he was training with other ticket agents, but for all I knew, he had decided not to take the job and headed back home to Deforest. I hoped not, though—I couldn't seem to shake his face from my mind, but unfortunately, I had no way of knowing if or when I'd see Nolan again.

Jack interrupted my thoughts. "So what are your plans for tonight?"

"Oh, I don't know," I replied. "Laura and I might go catch a movie if she doesn't have to work late. She's probably The Owl though." I knew my sister would most likely have to take the last boat tour of the night, and I'd be stuck at home with my parents, but I didn't want to sound lame. "How about you?"

"I hear there's a beer waiting for me down at the Sand Bar."

I shuddered at the thought of a dusty bottle hanging out on the grungy bar of the local hideaway downtown. Not sure why the tourists couldn't find this place, neatly tucked half a block off of Broadway, but most nights it was relatively void of Chicagoans and full of heartbroken locals.

"Jack, there's always a beer waiting for you down at the Sand Bar," I teased.

"Well, then that's the right place for me." A few thoughts rolled around his head for a moment. "You wanna join me tonight?"

"Aw, no thanks. You know my parents would kill me if I was down at the bar."

Jack replied with a shrug of his shoulders. "Suit yourself. More beer for me."

After we cleaned up the boat, I parted ways with Jack in the parking lot. Instead of hopping in my car and driving right home, something made me drift towards the overlook set just off the almost deserted parking lot. I sat down on one of the empty park benches facing the dock and the power dam, and placed my backpack right next to me.

The summer sun set behind my back, shining down over the steep cliff a few feet from my perch. A few of the gates on the dam were open and I watched as huge gushes of water cascaded over the cement walls. The soothing sounds coaxed me to close my eyes and take in a cleansing breath of the summer air.

Everything about the river was home to me. I hadn't realized how much I missed the unique sights and sounds while I was at college this past year, but a quiet moment of contentment next to my river set my heart at peace. I sat happily on that bench for what must have been almost ten minutes before I decided to go home and spend some time with my parents.

I stood, put on my heavy backpack, and turned to leave, but something shiny and blue caught my eye about five feet down the very steep hill in front of me. The beautiful, glittering object was hidden in a nest of overgrown grass and it piqued my interest. It looked a lot like a glowy blue rock I had found in a box in my parents' basement a few years ago. I had brought it up to my room, mesmerized by its odd beauty. I had never seen anything like it before, until now.

I leaned far over the long wooden safety barricade at my thighs, to get a better view. It looked as colorful as a little gem, but was very large—almost the size of an egg. It looked like the one on the shelf in my room, but this one was smaller.

Intent on the little blue rock, I swung my legs over the wooden fence, gripped the barricade with my left hand, and leaned down the steep hill, my right arm stretched out. My fingers were only a few inches from the gem, but the hill was so steep, and I knew I couldn't let go of the fence or I'd topple the sixty feet down the hill and into the deep and rushing waters of the Wisconsin River below.

Right as I was about to give up on my mysterious treasure, I decided to give it one more try. I reached again, causing the contents of my backpack to shift unexpectedly, sending my balance off-kilter. Surprised, I screamed and let go of the barricade in an attempt to catch my balance. My life moved in slow motion for the next few seconds as I fell forward, and I envisioned myself rolling down the rocky hill and crashing into the brown water below.

Before I could blink, two strong arms grabbed my backpack and yanked me on top of the barricade. I swung my legs over the fence and stood, thankful to be on solid ground.

"Nolan!" I breathed as I looked up at my hero. "You're here...I mean, you saved me!"

Oh my God.

His eyes were sparkling blue, but filled with worry. He dropped my hand quickly, but I could still feel the ghost of his touch on my skin.

"What were you doing? You could have fallen down that hill!"

He was mad at me. I didn't want him to be mad at me.

"I...I saw something shiny." Why did that sound so stupid when I said it out loud?

I looked over the hill, but my little blue orb was nowhere to be found. In my panic, I must have sent some loose rocks into the path of the beautiful treasure, sending it forever to the bottom of the deep river.

I turned back to Nolan. "How did...? Where did you...?" I couldn't form a sentence.

He started to back up a few steps. "I'm glad you're okay. I've gotta head to the Boat office," he said, pointing up the road. Then his frown turned to a smile. "Take care of yourself, Ava. I'd like to see you around here again."

No. Don't go.

Then he winked at me and left before I could crack out of my stunned silence.

That beautiful man just saved my life.

Chapter Three

"So, did you check your grades from last semester yet?" my best friend from college, Kasie, asked.

"Oh, are they out already?" I lied, taking a sip from the straw in my lemonade and switching my cell to the other ear. The evening summer sun was almost under the horizon. I loved sitting on my parents' front porch, watching the sun dip beneath the tree line.

"Ah, yeah. For about a week now! How could you not have checked?"

"I forgot." I was scared out of my pants to check my grades. I knew in my heart what they were, so why check? "I've been busy, I guess."

"You're a bad liar, Ava. Come clean."

"There's a hot new guy at work. I've been distracted!"

"New guy? Dish, girl."

"Well, he's handsome and somewhat mysterious. You know, someone who wouldn't go for a girl like me."

"What does that mean?" Kasie paused momentarily. "You have no idea your worth, do you?"

I smiled. Best friends were the breath of life. Maybe I didn't know how special I was, but at least I had friends who tried to convince me.

Kasie sighed at my silence and then scolded me. "You haven't seen Aaron, have you?"

"Calm down," I teased her. "I have not seen him. But this town isn't too big."

"Well, I hope he stays away. You need a break from that guy."

"I know." A tiny sliver of sun was all that was left of the day. A chilly June breeze ran up my bare legs and I tucked them under a light blanket. "How's work at the pool?"

"Not bad. I'm working on my tan sitting by the pool, getting hit on by mature guys all day!"

"Kasie, I've seen the clientele at the Stevens Point Community Pool. I think you're mistaking mature guys for men over eighty wearing too small swimwear."

She laughed loudly. "Fine! Busted! I think I'm going to have to pick up another shift so I can pay for tuition in the fall."

"I'm proud of you for working so hard."

"Thanks, Ava. Well, I should get going. It was good talking with you."

"Yeah, same here."

"Hey, check your grades. It's not too late to sign up for a summer term online course."

Ugh. I came home to get away from school and relax in my beloved Dells. School was the last thing I wanted to focus on this summer.

But instead I said, "Thanks, Kas. I'll think about it."

I hung up the phone and went right to a web browser. I put in my student ID into the UW–Stevens Point online grade book and hovered my finger over the log-in button. Nerves stirred in my stomach. I took a deep breath to calm them.

"Ava!" my mother called from inside the house. "Your dinner's ready!"

"Coming, Mom!" I yelled back. I closed the browser. My grades could wait until later.

* * * *

A few days after Nolan rescued me from my embarrassing stunt on the hill, I was more than thrilled when I caught sight of him in a booth called Lower One. He was training with expert ticket agent, Suzanne, and a guy I knew from high school, Brian.

Lower One was one of the largest ticket booths, complete with two ticket windows, green Astroturf carpeting, and oversized pictures of the Dells covering the walls. It was situated at the entrance to the grounds of the Lower Dells docks and was the best booth in town because it was constantly populated with people.

Jack and I stood at the dispatch booth, chatting with Rob. I could see Nolan across the way, laughing with Suzanne and Brian. My heart jumped into overdrive and my head spun. How could his heavenly smile get such a reaction out of me?

"Let's go hang out in the ticket booth, Jack." I had wanted to thank Nolan ever since he left me stunned a few days before.

"I'm game. I'm sure Suzanne is good for a laugh."

My nerves rumbled around as we snuck in the door and sat on the two captain's chairs in the back of the tiny booth, watching Suzanne, Brian, and Nolan sell tickets out of their windows.

Although Nolan was still in training, he seemed to be a natural at selling boat tickets. His charm and poise enabled him to sweet-talk anyone into buying tickets for both the Upper and Lower Dells tours. This was known as the complete tour, or "combo" to ticket agents, and it provided the biggest commission. Somehow, Nolan knew exactly what to say to each kind of tourist that arrived at his ticket window. I suspected that if he really wanted to, he could use his suavely crafted words and those beautiful baby blues to get some unsuspecting tourists to hand over their first born.

DBT owned several booths all over town with the intention of coaxing tourists on every corner of the city into taking a boat tour. Sixty years ago, ticket agents would jump into the streets of the Dells and even hang onto passing cars trying to solicit tourists to buy tickets. Now, of course, the agents had to wait for the tourists to approach the booths, and in order to be a good agent, you had to know how to talk the talk.

Most ticket agents were college kids who came home for the summer to make a few bucks and have a great time partying at the company's summer housing. The ticket booth at Lower One, however, was consistently inhabited by Suzanne, a veteran agent well out of college who sported a cropped hairstyle and a taste for noticeably inappropriate jokes.

In the off-season, she spent her winters subbing at the high school in town, although I couldn't imagine her leading a class full of teenagers anywhere besides down the wrong road. She was joined daily with another agent in the booth at Lower One, and together they would stay busy shelling out combos the entire day.

Jack and I often spent our breaks hanging out in the booth listening to Suzanne and Brian goof around, so it wasn't anything out of the ordinary for us to show up on the chairs in the back. I was trying to figure out how I could have a private conversation with Nolan in the booth while everyone else was there. I was sure I didn't want the others to know about my ridiculous brush with death, but I needed to thank Nolan.

Suzanne engaged in conversation with us the moment we entered, but Brian and Nolan were busy with customers. When the old couple left Nolan's window, he turned around, smiling at me, and walked right over to my side. Suzanne continued talking with Jack; it was my one chance.

"Ava. It's so good to see you." His smile was intoxicating.

"I'm so sorry about the other day," I said nervously. "I can't thank you enough for what you did."

"It was my pleasure," Nolan said sweetly. But then his expression changed quickly. "But it was not my pleasure believing you were about to plummet to your death. Do you normally take such inappropriate risks?"

I laughed loudly to cover my embarrassment. "No. I'm not normally a risk taker, I just..." My mind raced back to that stupid little glittery rock. "Never mind. It doesn't matter." I smiled, suddenly lost in Nolan's eyes.

He placed his hand on my shoulder momentarily as if to say, "I forgive you."

Something electric stirred inside me. I could feel the warmth of his hand radiating through my thin work shirt.

Some more customers came up to the windows and Nolan's hand drifted off my shoulder too soon. Just like that the three ticket agents were hard at work again. I lifted my hand up to the spot where Nolan's had just been, but Jack pulled on my elbow.

"Come on, we've gotta go sweep before our next trip."

I reluctantly slid off the chair, unable to bid Nolan goodbye as Jack dragged me out of the ticket booth.

* * * *

As the days went on, I convinced Jack to hang out in the ticket booth several times a day, but about a week later, unhappily to me, Jack revealed that he felt the tiny booth was too small for five people and wanted us to find a new hangout space.

I disagreed, but for some reason didn't want to tell Jack how I felt about Nolan, despite the truth that I simply couldn't get him out of my mind.

It was incredibly difficult to judge Nolan's feelings for me, however, because his naturally flirty personality made it appear as though he was hitting on basically anyone he came into contact with: elderly ladies, children, hot twenty-somethings, and everyone in between.

I tried to tell myself it was all stupid, anyway. Was I ready to jump into a relationship with someone right now? My heart still felt like it was in a million pieces after my last boyfriend, Aaron, was done with me and my faith in love had completely crumbled.

On the other hand, there was no denying the jolt of life I felt every time I was within a few feet of Nolan.

Darren spotted Nolan's talent early on and scheduled him frequently in the best booths. Nolan had completed his training, and I was happy to see him at work almost every day. Time made my mysterious connection with Nolan that much stronger. With our comfortable conversations and benign flirting in the booth, we were definitely passing from friendship into perhaps something more. I was still cautious, but with each encounter I started to feel a tiny flame of excitement rekindling my heart.

After the last tourist hopped off the back of my boat one afternoon in mid-June, I waited the right amount of time for them to head for the exit, and then I raced up the stairs by dispatch to visit Nolan in the corner booth again. I hoped Suzanne had headed home early so Nolan and I could spend a few minutes alone together before my last tour of the day. My heart skipped a beat as I approached the booth and saw only him leaning up against the counter on the opposite side of the booth. Careful not to make too much noise, I approached the booth quietly, hoping to sneak up on him. When I got close enough I realized he was talking on the phone, but what was that I heard? It sounded like he was speaking a foreign language, like maybe Russian. Curious, I slipped in the back door and sat down on a stool just as he hung up the phone. He turned his head over his shoulder, saw me, and then flashed that captivating smile. A pleasant tingle slid through my body, making me forget all about the weird phone call.

"So, Miss Ava, can't stay away, huh?" he teased. This was my fourth trip to the ticket booth today. Were my cheeks the color I felt they were? I surely looked like a fool! I tried to wipe them inconspicuously with the back of my hand, as if that would do something to help.

"Jack wanted to run to the bank before our 5:15 tour and I've already swept the top deck, so I thought I'd come up here and keep you company. Where's Suzanne?" I tried to nonchalantly thumb the rack of brochures on the counter.

He backed into the corner of the triangle-shaped booth and hoisted himself up on the counter. It looked like something my mother would scold me for doing on the kitchen counter. "She ran out to her car to get me the schedule for next week. She'll be right back."

Damn.

"Is the 5:15 your last trip? I've gotta work until eight tonight." He looked up at me, and I tried not to dive into the tranquil seas above his nose, but I got lost beneath his long eyelashes.

"Ava...are you alright? You've got the weirdest expression on your face."

Dammit! Play it cool, girl!

"Yeah, sorry. We had two back-to-backs, and I didn't really get a chance to eat lunch today." It was only a half-truth. I did eat a snack-sized bag of mini pretzels on the way back upriver during the last tour.

"Hold down the fort here, and I'll run back to the Last Chance to get you something." He hopped off the counter that rounded the booth and was silently closing in the gap between us.

His chest looked like the most perfect place to rest the side of my head. To invite his arms to wrap around me like two satin ribbons, pull me in close, and tie gently behind my back.

Like an idiot, I let out an involuntary sigh.

Oops. Did he hear that?

"Hey, Queenie! Where's Captain Jack?" Suzanne barged through the door and quickly freed me from the trance Nolan was holding me in.

"Why do you call her Queenie, anyway?" Nolan asked Suzanne, not breaking eye contact with me.

I pleaded with her, "Oh, no. Please, Suzanne..." This could be embarrassing. There were some things I wasn't ready to share with Nolan yet. I closed my eyes.

"Oh, don't you know?" An amused smile graced her lips. "I do a little subbing up at the high school, and three years ago when our little Ava here was a junior, she was elected prom queen."

"Ah! Well, that explains a lot." Nolan, grinning widely from ear to ear, walked back over to the corner spot.

"And what exactly does that mean?" I played along, letting my hands land on my hips in protest.

Suzanne laughed and held one finger up in the air. "Oh wait, honey, there's more. As a senior she was named Homecoming Queen. That's right. Prom *and* Homecoming Queen. I'd say we've got royalty amongst us!" Then she slapped me on the knee like a move from some hoedown dance.

The corners of Nolan's mouth turned up slowly.

"No, I did not sleep with half the class, as I can tell you're thinking. Let's just say I am a very friendly and sweet person. It's in my blood. A family trait, you could say."

"I'm sure you are." A hardly innocent and crooked smile swept across his face, but somehow I still liked it.

Suzanne let out a loud belly laugh, and a baby near the booth began to cry.

* * * *

The next day Nolan was assigned to a different ticket booth uptown. Suzanne made a tiara in my honor out of the tinfoil from her lunch and posted it on top of the clock in the booth. Nolan would think that was quite funny. It was a very slow day, but I couldn't tell if it was from the lack of tourists or because my Nolan wasn't around.

I spent time between boats thinking about checking my grades. Several times I had the page up on my phone, waiting for me to press log-in.

"Just do it," Jack pressured me. "I can't imagine them being that bad. Not from you."

I swung around to see him peering over my shoulder. "You have no idea."

"You? Bad grades? Come on, what classes did you take?"

"English 101, Intro to Psychology, Chem lab, and US History 110."

"Well, see there's the problem. Those are boring. Where's your teaching classes?"

"I can't take teaching courses until I'm admitted into the School of Education." I sat down on the back deck of the *Bailey*. "And I can't get into the School of Ed unless I have good grades."

"Then get good grades!"

I blew a raspberry at him and he laughed. "You make it sound so easy."

"Just check 'em."

Passengers began to descend the stairs and down onto the blue dock. "Later," I said, tucking my phone away. "I've got a tour to give."

"Right on!" Jack said, taking his place at the back of the boat. "All aboard!" he yelled.

* * * *

On Wednesday Nolan was finally back at Lower One. Once the last tourist walked off my boat from my first tour, I wanted desperately to push through the crowd, scale the stairs two at a time, and run back to that corner booth. But I knew I needed to restrain myself as well as I could. Jack told me he had to fuel up the boat and asked if I'd run up to the Last Chance Snack Stand to buy him some Rolos.

"Take it out of my tips, kid. If we have any." He tried to smile, but I knew he was completely serious.

Glad for an excuse to leave the dock, I took the stairs to the dispatch booth maybe too quickly for DBT safety regulations and breathlessly said hi to Rob as I passed by. I walked right by the Last Chance, thinking I'd buy the candy on my way back down to the dock. I needed a Nolan-fix as soon as possible, but as I rounded the corner, I saw only Suzanne standing in the triangle booth. I stood there stuck for a moment. I didn't really want to go hang out with Suzanne, but she caught me curiously peeking around the corner for Nolan.

"He's not here!" I heard Suzanne yell in a singsongy voice.

Shoot!

"Okay," was all I managed to squeak out. What do I do now? Was it rude to turn around and walk away?

Before I could tell my feet to move she continued, "But he asked me to give you this." She held out a piece of white paper folded in half. She shook it teasingly out the open window, gently drawing me in. A note? What, were we in junior high? Even so, I smiled widely and took three very excited skips toward the booth.

Stop, idiot! I must look ridiculous, so I slowed it down to a casual walk.

I grabbed for the paper, but she pulled it away quickly and held it up near her face, which was hosting the strangest grin. "So, Queenie...what's with you and Nolan?"

My cheeks burned with embarrassment. My voice was stuck—I couldn't say anything! "What do you mean?"

"I mean, the kid doesn't stop talking about you."

He doesn't?

I stood there, smiling like an idiot, and then reached up and gleefully took the note from her hands. I could feel Suzanne peering over my shoulder and turned forty degrees right so she couldn't see, although I knew she had read it already anyway.

Hey kiddo. They moved me out to Delton Corners for the day. I have to work until 8. You should stop by when you're off work.

Nolan

He wants me to stop by.

"I think you should go out there and see what he wants," Suzanne said. "He's a handsome guy, you know, and if I were twenty years younger I'd have already bagged that hot piece!" Then Suzanne laughed her boisterous laugh, and I walked away shaking my head, slightly disturbed.

Chapter Four

My heart was racing as I pulled my baby blue Oldsmobile into the parking lot at Delton Corners. Delton Corners was the ticket booth owned by DBT located farthest from the docks. Lake Delton was a small town butted right up against the city of Wisconsin Dells. There were attractions in both towns, and many tourists probably never knew they crossed the lines into another town when they drove down Highway 12.

I turned the keys in the ignition and pulled them out. Suddenly, I felt a sharp stab behind my left eyeball. "Ow! What the heck?" But then the pain was gone as quickly as it had come on.

"Weird." I rubbed my eye for a few seconds until I was sure the pain was gone, and then I looked up at the ticket booth. I could barely see Nolan's face behind the wall of closed windows. I took a deep breath, held it for a few too many seconds, and then let it fly loudly out of my mouth.

I sat fiddling with my keys, waiting for my head to tell my hands to open the door. Why couldn't I move?

After several seconds, I finally pulled down the visor and checked my appearance in the mirror. *Hmm, not my best.* But then again, I did just finish a seven-tour day—what did he expect? If I was lucky, he found the wind-blown look sexy.

Delton Corners was the largest ticket booth DBT owned. It was the size of a small living room with rows and rows of windows and a small ticket counter several feet from the front door. I nervously walked in the back door—and there he was, facing the row of windows out the front of the booth. He looked like he was about to do some kind of goofy dance, like he was hearing some kind of funky music in his head.

What was I doing out in the middle of nowhere with this guy? I barely know him!

I started backing up toward the door...he hadn't noticed me yet. But as my head was telling me to abort the mission, my heart was telling me to move forward and explore a little more. He must have heard my heart beating out of my chest because he suddenly turned around.

"Couldn't stay away, huh?" His smile was as radiant as the sun. He was blinding me with his straight teeth and icy blue eyes. The sight of Nolan's muscled shoulders and arms bulging through the white boat shirt began to stir up something exciting inside of me.

"Yeah, well, Suzanne passed me a note after study hall," I teased, "so I figured I had to come see what you wanted." I could feel sweat building up in my palms.

Stay cool, girl, stay cool.

I looked away quickly to the floor—I couldn't get pulled in again. My brain turned to mush whenever that happened.

"I'm really happy you came out here. I wanted to see you again." Nolan put his tablet under the counter and came around to the other side.

"I'll see you at Lower One tomorrow, won't I?" Did I have the courage to ask what I really wanted to? I suddenly felt like I wanted to see him every second of the day.

"Yeah. I guess you will." His eyes were staring at me again. My stomach felt as though it were on fire while my heart felt like it was playing a circus march on steroids. It was the most wonderful feeling. I thought I'd never feel like this again after graduation last spring.

For my last two blissful years of high school, I dated the quarterback of the football team and local hottie, Aaron. But last year when we graduated, he dumped me as we headed off to different colleges. Breaking up came as quite a shock to my heart because I really thought I was going to marry him. After a year of reflection, I realized that probably most girls who fall in love with their high school boyfriends think they have found "the one."

It's a wonder how I made it through my first year at UW–Stevens Point without falling into a deep depression. Aaron showed up at the door of my heart, calling, emailing, and teasing me with the temptation of getting back together. He also showed up at the door of my dorm on several occasions, sending me joyfully back into love with him, only to leave me lonely again. Each time, when I thought he'd found a place for me in his heart, he'd stop talking to me for weeks at a time. At some point last spring, he decided it was unhealthy to keep going back and forth like that, and he broke it off for good.

Before I knew it, two whole semesters of college has passed like a blur across my brain.

I knew this summer could end up being awkward since we were both going to be working in the Dells for three months. But I hadn't seen Aaron at all this summer. He was a driver and tour guide for the Original Wisconsin Ducks. The Ducks was one of the most popular attractions in the Dells, aside from the waterparks. For a small fortune, you could take your family aboard an authentic, WWII vehicle called a Duck. The big, army green, twenty-passenger truck drove through the forests around the Dells and then thrilled its passengers as it plunged directly into the Wisconsin River and magically transformed into a boat.

The Duck entrance at Echo Point was right around the turn near the beginning of the Lower Dells Boat Tour, and every time I rounded that corner, my heart skipped a beat, as I was hoping to see Dolly, the Duck Aaron drove. Although each time I secretly wanted it to be Aaron, it didn't really matter because the Duck company seemed to hire only good-looking college men in their twenties, and I was happy to flirtatiously wave at any one of them.

I was still somewhat infatuated with Aaron when I came home from college for the summer. I never really got an answer to what went wrong in our relationship, and I blamed myself somehow. Now I wondered if anyone could ever love me the way Aaron once did. Could I really now be finding a way to break free from the hold Aaron had on my heart? My mind came back to the present, and somehow Nolan was only a few feet away from me.

How did he move so quickly without me knowing?

He randomly picked a brochure for the Tommy Bartlett Ski Show off the rack and nervously rolled it into a tube. "So, how was your day?"

Something told me this wasn't a good idea. Why risk heartache again?

I pulled my tongue out of the back of my throat and squeaked out, "Fine. We sold books."

Dammit! Why did he come off so smooth while I sounded like an idiot?

He gave a chuckle under his breath. "That's good." He moved in closer, and I could smell his cologne. The scent just about tipped me right off my feet when he suddenly stopped his momentum, turned on the spot, and headed back over to the ticket counter.

I snapped out of his delicious scent-hold and wondered what I did wrong. I turned and breathed into my hand for a quick breath check. Was my hair more hideous than I had thought?

He stayed at the counter, doing something by the till. It was odd behavior.

"Well, I have to get going. My parents will be expecting me." I started backing out of the booth, still facing him, unable to turn away. The next few seconds passed in slow motion as my foot smashed into the corner of a metal stand holding up the American flag. The flag crashed to the floor with a loud clang and I flew backwards, grabbing the rack of brochures to break my fall. But it didn't. The papers went flying through the air as I landed on my right hip on the concrete floor, covered in brochures for Dells attractions and a metal rack on my chest.

Oh my God. Did that really just happen?

Nolan jumped up from his spot at the counter and ran over to my side. He dug me out of the pile of brightly colored papers, asking if I was okay.

That was it. I just ruined my chances to spend any time with this cool, alluring boy this summer. Who would want to be with "Ava the Clumsy"? I was mortified and wanted nothing more than to hide in the cave of brochures on top of me and never see Nolan again.

I opened my eyes and found his blue eyes not more than four inches before me. His breath on my face confirmed the lack of space between us.

Three beats of silence passed as we searched each other's eyes for answers, and then a tiny chuckle escaped Nolan's mouth. He tightened his lips, trying to hold it back, but it was so cute I collapsed into laughter. Relief played on his face as he offered a hand to help me up, and we laughed comfortably for a minute together.

I knew right then no matter what happened this summer, I'd never forget the time Nolan watched me pick a fight with a brochure rack.

Chapter Five

Twenty minutes later I parked the Olds in front of my parents' house on Capital Street, walked up the sidewalk and through the front door.

My mom was an elementary music teacher and spent her summers working in the garden, sitting on church committees, quilting, and reading. My father had always worked in the bank industry. I didn't really know exactly what he did, only that he had climbed his way to the top and now sat as the head of some rather rare Midwestern chain I could never remember the name of. In fact, there wasn't one of his banks in the county, and Dad had to travel as far as Madison or Milwaukee almost daily. Although he was extremely busy and often spent time traveling for work, when my sister and I were growing up he always made sure to be home to tuck us in for bed most nights of the week. He saved all his vacation days so he could take a few weeks off during the summer to spend time with his wife and daughters. I had a feeling my mother never really liked Dad's job arrangement, but she supported him just the same.

Mom had a plate of supper already in the microwave when I entered the kitchen. "How was your day, honey? Did you have any full boats?" Mom brought over a bowl of reheated spaghetti and a tall glass of milk. She sat down in the chair next to me and sipped on a glass of ice water.

"One at noon, but otherwise pretty slow." I took out my wad of money that was now considerably smaller since I gave half of it to Jack. I stood up from the table and took it over to my dad, who was sitting on the couch in the adjoining living room watching *Jeopardy*. He loved to count every bill my sister and I brought home—banking was probably in his blood. "Sorry, Dad, not too much to flash around today. Where's Laura?"

"She had to take The Owl." Dad was flipping bills around so they were all facing the same way. My sister, Laura, was an Upper Dells guide. She really wanted to become a pilot, though, and was coaxing her boat driver to teach her tips on docking every day. Although Laura was one year younger than me, she was taller and smarter. She was beautiful and full of confidence. I knew she'd one day become one of the best female pilots the Upper Dells had ever seen.

I had finished my spaghetti and was taking the plate to the sink just as the doorbell rang.

"I'll get it, Mom." An excited jolt ran through my body. Could Nolan be at my door? No, why would I think that? He had no idea where I lived.

I opened the front door and my stomach instantly dropped.

"Aaron?"

My ex-boyfriend stood at the bottom of the concrete stairs outside of my parents' front porch. He was wearing his summer uniform—army green Duck shorts and a tucked-in white polo with the company's logo embroidered on the left breast. He had his hands in his pockets and looked at the ground, moving his feet back and forth anxiously.

"What are you doing here, Aaron?"

"Ava," he said, looking up at me finally. "Can I talk to you?"

I stayed on the top stair, but shut the porch door behind me. "I'm not sure I have anything to say to you."

"Listen. I'm sorry about how things ended a few months ago."

Angry memories of the last year flickered in front of my mind's eye like scenes from a film reel. I had spent too much time agonizing over the state of the relationship with my first failed love.

Then, unexpectedly, I saw a vision of Nolan and felt something warm in my heart.

"I don't need your apologies. Have a great summer, Aaron. I'll see you around."

I turned towards the house and placed my hand on the door handle.

"Wait." Aaron made up the space between us quickly and placed his hand on top of mine.

Shaking, I turned around to face him. His familiar green eyes penetrated mine. I involuntarily relived the sweet memories of our time in high school together. It was one of the happiest times of my life.

"I miss you," he breathed. His was slowly moving in towards me.

I was so confused. Was this what I wanted?

No. Heartache. He's nothing but heartache.

"Ava." Aaron slid his hand around my waist, to my lower back. It felt so nice to be touched again. To be held tightly by a man. His other hand found my neck, his thumb gently rubbing the sensitive place under my ears. I closed my eyes, surrendering to the pleasant feelings rushing back to me.

I was well aware of his face inching closer and closer to mine, but found little will to send him away. Maybe this was what I wanted.

"I still love you," he whispered right before his lips touched mine.

I kissed him back for a quick second. But the physicality of it jolted my logical brain into action. Getting back together with Aaron was not a good idea.

"No!" I pulled back quickly. "Aaron. You need to go. It's over between us. Forever."

"Aw, sweetie," he pulled my waist in closer to his, "you don't mean that. Think of all the good times we spent together."

I squirmed in his arms, trying to break free, but he was too strong.

"Let go of me!" I screamed.

"You're my girl, Ava." He grabbed my wrists and squeezed too hard as I tried to yank them free. "I need you."

Panic began to fill my heart. "Ow," I whined. "You're hurting me!"

He released me a little, but still gripped my wrists and stood close.

"I can't live without you. Please..."

"Aaron, let go!" I whined again, trying to hit him with my fists.

"Hey!" someone called from the middle of the street. "She said let go!"

Footsteps quickly ran up the sidewalk, and then I heard Aaron grunt and he released me, falling suddenly to the ground.

"Ava, are you alright?"

It was Nolan. On my front steps. Punching out my ex-boyfriend.

My jaw dropped. Where did he come from?

Aaron scrambled to his feet and swung wildly at Nolan, missing horribly. Nolan pulled some kind of fancy move, catching Aaron's arm and using it as a lever to flip Aaron over his head and flat to the ground, stunned.

It looked like it came right out of a movie.

Chests heaving, they stared at each other for a moment and I wondered what would happen next. Blood trickled from Aaron's nose onto my parent's front lawn, and then he got up, ran to his car and drove off.

Nolan was back at my side, his hand on my upper arm. "Are you hurt?"

I shook my head, still stunned.

"Who was that jerk?"

"My ex-boyfriend." I took a deep breath and let it out. Then I met his eyes, full of concern. "That was scary. Thanks."

"You're welcome. Don't worry about him. I bet he won't be coming by anymore."

"Where did you learn to fight like that?"

"Oh, I don't know. Must have been the karate I took as a kid."

"Obviously," I said, trying to laugh through all the emotions racing through me. I let my knees sink with relief and I sat down on the front steps. Nolan joined me.

"You're not okay. You're shaking."

Get a hold of yourself, Ava!

"I'm fine."

"How is it, might I ask, that you always happen to be right within reach when I need help?" I smiled, trying to hide my nervousness. "Are you stalking me, sir?"

"It would seem so, wouldn't it?" He smiled adorably. "The truth is, I've just discovered I'm your neighbor for the summer." He pointed across the street to the cabins across the alley in the next block over.

"Boat Tours housing? I should have known."

"You should come over sometime and see my digs."

My heart smiled along with my lips. "You know, I'd like that."

"How about tomorrow? After work? You're the local. You could come see my cabin and then take me around to all the best spots in town."

Excitement mixed with nerves coursed through my veins. "Sure. Sounds great."

Nolan stood up to leave.

"Thanks again, Nolan."

"My pleasure." His bright smile melted my heart. "Goodnight, Ava."

"Goodnight, Nolan."

I watched him cross the street, turning back once to wave at me. He trekked through the lawn of the houses on the other side and then crossed the alley and into Animal Island. A wonderful feeling filled my heart. I was going on a date with Nolan Hill.

I stopped at the front door because I heard my parents quietly arguing in the living room on the other side of the door—an act uncharacteristic of their marriage. I knew eavesdropping was wrong, but I couldn't help myself.

"He's been off the map for almost fifteen years, Kate," my father said. "We have to ask ourselves—why now?"

"I haven't got a clue, but I have a bad feeling about this." Mom sounded worried, and I had no idea what they were talking about. "George. Please don't go," she said.

"I'm sorry, honey, but I have to." Dad lowered his voice and said something I couldn't hear.

"How can you be so sure?" Mom asked.

"This is our family we're talking about. I told you all those years ago, and I still hold firm on this—I will not risk my family's safety."

My mother let out a loud sigh of disapproval. "Fine. I'll support you if that's what you want." Mom walked away from the conversation, and I heard my father grunt softly.

What was that about?

Chapter Six

Jack asked for a few extra days off. "Some family thing up North," he told me the day before. So I was stuck with awful Captain Dean. Dean was a very tall man with square shoulders, graying hair, and boxy, oversized glasses. He somehow reminded me of a bald eagle. He was also a schoolteacher, although I could not imagine him teaching any children, as one look from his rigid, tight face would scare any child. It sent chills down my spine, and I was nineteen years old for goodness sake.

I also believed Dean suffered from OCD. He expected his guide to be at work forty-five minutes early to wash the windows with a specific formula he made himself, and to "wipe it off in a clockwise direction," using only a cotton blend towel. After that, each life vest belt had to be checked and neatly placed in straight rows behind the chairs on the bottom deck. These were chores none of the other crews did. Well, at least not regularly.

I carefully walked aboard that morning and made my way to the front of the boat to deposit my workbag. A roll of paper towels and a bottle of Windex were sitting suggestively on the guide's side of the dash. I sighed and got to work wiping down the chairs on the bottom deck while Dean was busy with the windows in the back.

He cordially greeted me good morning and then informed me that we only had thirty minutes before our first tour, and I should make sure the garbage cans on the top and back deck were wiped down. After I had completed all the random and completely useless jobs he required me to do, I decided to hit the restroom before our first trip.

Dean made quite a few remarks of "positive criticism" on each of my first two tours and only asked me to wipe down the rails on the upper deck twice that day. As if working with crazy Captain Dean wasn't enough, Nolan was stationed at an uptown booth, so I couldn't even spend my breaks with him.

One trip, on the way back up river, I tried to strike up a conversation with Dean about teaching. But I soon realized it was a mistake, as Dean turned out to be very uninspired in the classroom and didn't like his job much at all. As he jabbered on about the politics of his district, I daydreamed about my not so stellar first year at UWSP.

"You'll have to work harder to prepare yourself for the next exam, Miss Gardner," my History professor had told me as she handed back my test. A large F was written in red ink on the top of my paper. The sight of it stopped my heart for what felt like a full thirty seconds. It was my first F on a test. Ever.

I slipped the test into my backpack with shaking hands.

"I lead a study group that meets every Thursday evening on the second floor of the library. I suggest you attend."

"Thanks," I muttered as I got up from my chair. I held back my tears until I was clear of the crowd leaving the classroom. I craved my mother's arms to hold me and for her to tell me it would be okay. College was a lonely place—so many people and no one familiar enough to cry to. I wandered the campus for an hour, wondering what I was doing there. Maybe college wasn't the place for me. But what else was I to do with my life?

Finally I arrived at my dorm room and called Aaron right away.

"It's just one F, baby. You'll be fine."

I sniffled, crying quietly.

"Want me to come over? I'll make you feel better."

"Aaron, you're three hours away." But I wanted really badly for him to come. I needed him.

"I'm leaving now, baby. I'll be there by 8 tonight."

But he never came. I got a text at 8:30 saying something came up and he wasn't going to be able to make it. Then I didn't hear from him for three weeks.

Kasie said she'd kick his ass if he came near me again. But a month later he showed up at our door with a bouquet of flowers. Kasie knew he made me happy, if only temporarily, so she let him in and I skipped study group that night.

I always knew I wanted to be a teacher, so I spent time volunteering in a first grade classroom during my last year of high school. All aspects of high school came easily to me, and I graduated with decent grades and social ranking. I headed off to college high on life, but the academics turned out to be much tougher than I had expected and I soon realized I had never really learned how to study. My dreams of teaching started to deflate with each poor grade I earned, and I began to wonder if maybe I didn't have an ounce of teacher inside me.

Although I made some great girlfriends, I missed being popular and the dramatic rollercoaster ride with Aaron left me more than distracted. For once, my world was shaken, and I had craved the solace of the Dells to help me refocus and recharge for the challenges of the next year of my life.

The day drifted by utterly slowly, and I had a lot of time to think about what I had overheard my parents discussing the night before. That morning, my mom told me Dad had to go on a business trip and would be gone for a few days. The sad look on my mom's face scared me. Perhaps it wasn't simply a marital squabble. I carefully asked my mom if everything was okay, but she threw on a happy face and assured me all was fine. It was all very mysterious, but I trusted my parents to work everything out on their own.

Before I knew it, I was released from Dean's laser eyes and off to the parking lot. I passed Brian in the front ticket booth on my way out and decided to stop for a quick chat. Brian and I had been classmates in high school. We were friendly enough, but didn't end up in the same social circles.

"Hey Ava. How'd you survive the day with Captain Scary?"

"Ah, yes. I barely survived. I think my hands still smell like Windex." I held my fingers up for him to sniff, but he didn't.

"What are you up to tonight?" Brian seemed to have an instigator's smile on his lips, and I knew he had been talking to Suzanne.

"Yes, it is true—I am going on a date with Nolan. Have you gotten to work alone with him yet?" I asked.

"Yeah, a few times. Seems like a nice guy. Funny as hell, you know." He paused for a moment and looked me in the eyes. "Now, Ava. Don't let that boy take advantage of you! You keep your sweet little self wholesome, will ya?"

"Of course, Brian. Would you expect anything else from me?" I left the booth and walked out to my car with a smile on my face that just wouldn't go away. When my friend Jules met her husband in college, she was so happy she said she had a perma-smile. I liked my perma-smile now and wished it would stay forever.

When I got home, I showered and then stared at my closet for too many minutes wondering what I should wear. I settled on a pair of white shorts and a clingy, plain black V-neck T-shirt. I blow-dried and straightened my hair, put on a bit of eye shadow and mascara, and then sprayed on a spritz of "Dream" by Gap to close the deal.

I found my mom in the kitchen. "Wow! You look great! Going out with the boys tonight?"

For most of my high school career, I spent the summers hanging out with Aaron and his two friends, Ted and Joel. We were a veritable four peas in a pod until Aaron broke up with me last year. Since then, it has been a case of choosing sides for Ted and Joel. Hang out with Aaron or Ava? I seemed to be losing the battle more often than not, but I couldn't blame them, I guess.

"I'm going out with *a* boy." I waited for her to catch on.

She put down the wooden spoon and turned towards me with a hand on her hip. "And which boy would this be? Someone I know?"

"Actually you don't know him. His name is Nolan Hill, and he is a new ticket agent at the Boats." I could see the trepidation in her eyes. "He's a very nice boy, Mom."

"Well, I should hope so as you deserve nothing less." She grabbed my shoulders and kissed my forehead. "Have fun and be home before 12:30." I hated that I had a curfew. I was not used to that at college, but my mother said as long as I was living under her roof, I'd have to respect her rules.

Fair enough—free rent.

It was finally about date time, so I perched myself behind the window in the living room. I could see between the two houses across the street and into the Dells Boat Tours housing. Companies throughout the Dells frequently hired foreign students to fill their summer positions. They often needed to provide housing for these students, so many companies bought out old, rundown motels around town and rented the rooms to these students. The Boats bought an old, two-story house that had six very small cabins on its land. There was a lawn with a campfire area amongst the cabins where parties frequently broke out. Someone nailed an old sign to the tree out front that said "*Animal Island.*" Aptly named.

I let my eyes relax as I stared out of the window. Soon my vision became blurry, and in a matter of seconds, the lawn and cabins across the way started to pixelate into large squares like the river had the day before. It was like someone took a picture of my view and then blew it up too large and it became unfocused. I blinked several times and rubbed my eyes, but the squares began to pulse like some sort of hypnotist's trick. When I blinked again, the view became focused, sharp as ever. I blinked a few more times to make sure the view was clear.

Could I be stressed? Does nervousness affect the eyes?

I only looked out the window for a few more seconds when, soon enough, Nolan left his cabin. I watched him walk out the door and sniff his armpits. I laughed at his moment of insecurity. So perhaps he wasn't as perfect as I thought. He kicked a half charred log in the fire pit, checked his watch, and then walked into the alley. I watched him turn onto the sidewalk and walk down to the next corner. I jumped down the stairs to meet him, and when I opened the door, he was walking past the split rail fence on our property.

"Hey there, stranger. Man, what a long walk," he joked. "I can't believe we live so close to each other. This is hilarious!"

"I know! So, do you want to come in and meet my parents?"

"Wow. Meeting the parents on the first date." An awkward silence followed, and I was about to retract my statement when he looked up at me and sincerely replied, "That sounds wonderful. Parents love me."

I smiled at him and opened up the porch door. "Do you want the grand tour?"

"Of course!" he said and followed me through the dining room.

"This is the formal dining room, which we hardly use." We walked past the upright piano pushed up against the wall and into the kitchen. Then I pointed into the family room and over to the bathroom and my sister's room.

We walked back through the rooms we had already traveled through and I led him up the stairs. The small bathroom was off to our left, and then I pointed down the hall and told him my parents' room was at the end.

"This looks like a great place to call home. Have you lived here all your life?" he asked. I loved how he always seemed so interested in everything about me.

"Yes, my parents have lived in this house for twenty-one years." Then I led him through the door to my bedroom. He took some time looking around at the pictures on the bookshelf and asked me who a few of the people were. I didn't want him to get any ideas about me bringing him to my bedroom, so I grabbed my purse and told him we better get going.

I led him back downstairs to the living room where we found my mother reading. "Hey, Mom. This is Nolan. He is a ticket agent at the boats, and we're going to go catch a movie." My mother put her book down and turned towards us. Nolan already had his arm extended and was shaking my mother's hand before I knew it. His deep, blue eyes focused intently on her face, and he was expertly making small talk as I watched. My mother wished us a good night, and I led Nolan out the front of the house. I was impressed—that was perfect.

I pulled my keys out and unlocked the passenger side door to the Oldsmobile. "Don't make fun of my car. I inherited it from my grandmother when she passed away a few years ago."

Nolan climbed in the front seat. "Make fun? This car is awesome! It's got character!" I slid the keys into the ignition and put the car in drive. It gave a very scary rumble but then jumped violently forward. Nolan slammed into the front dash. "Wait until I've got my seatbelt on next time!" he said laughing. "Well, it is unique, that's for sure!"

I laughed lightly, slightly embarrassed.

He looked a little disappointed. "So we're going to the movies? I thought you were going to show me all the local hotspots."

"I only said that so my mom would stay off my back. I didn't think she'd like it if I told her I was taking you to Make Out Rock." I slowly smiled and looked carefully over to Nolan's face as it sunk in. It was priceless.

"Where are you taking me? Now hold on here, little lady! I don't know who you think you are, but you can't just take me to some rock and have your way with me. I have high morals, you know!" But I knew he was kidding because that flirty, crooked smile came out again.

I decided to play along. "I'm sorry I misjudged you, sir. I'll adjust my schedule to accommodate your moral upbringing." My perma-smile was making another appearance, and I was pretty sure my checks were apple red again.

He laughed. "So where are you taking me for real?" he asked slyly. Dark green Wisconsin pines sped by on both sides of the car.

"It's a secret," I said and continued down the road. Nolan only grinned. I could tell he was loving it. About a mile later, I pulled the car off to the side of the road. "Get out," I instructed him.

He looked at the forest of pine trees that surrounded the road. "Um...where are we going? Should I be scared? This whole scenario reminds me of a slasher movie I watched last week." He stood by his door, waiting for further instruction as it truly did look like there was no reason for us to be visiting this remote location. I walked around the back of the car, and then gave Nolan a playful punch on the shoulder. "Come on, follow me."

We had arrived at the end of Bowman road. He followed me down a short dirt path through the woods and joined me on top of a tremendous sandstone cliff overlooking the peaceful, winding river. The gleaming sun set in front of us, and an orange glow sparkled off the chocolate brown water. The surface was quiet and still except for the edges as they gently licked the blonde, sandy beaches below. The towering, rocky cliffs seemed to be radiating warmth onto us. There wasn't a boat on the river. There wasn't a cloud in the sky. It was as if we were the last two people left on earth. I could hear nothing except an occasional wave upon the shore and the loud beating of my heart.

It was my favorite spot to come to alone, and now I was sharing it with someone I felt special about. Something sweetly touched my hand, and as I glanced down I saw Nolan's fingers intertwine with mine. The feeling of his hand sent a million tiny sparks jumping through my hand and up my arm. I felt so ecstatic that I felt we could fly through the air if we only took the leap. We said nothing for a few minutes until a hawk broke the silence. It glided smoothly through the air upon its impressive wingspan until it landed on a tree branch downriver from us.

"Thank you for bringing me here," Nolan said to me as he squeezed my hand. He turned to face me and searched my face with his beautiful eyes. "This is the best date I've ever been on."

A smile graced its way onto my face, and I replied, "But it just got started." I stared back at the winding river below us. "You know, the Winnebago had their own creation story on how this river came to be." I looked at him and noticed his eyes willing me to go on. "They believed a great serpent came down from the north and pushed its way through the Wisconsin countryside. When it wiggled and slithered through the soft sandstone, its body created the twisting riverbed and water rushed in behind it. Tiny snakes fled, terrified, from its path and created the small tributaries and waterways on the Wisconsin today."

"Fascinating," was all he could say. Most men would want to move on with the date and turn to hop back into the car at this point. But I realized that Nolan was someone special. He stayed to take in the view, to really breathe it in and immerse himself in this piece of nature that I truly loved. He was interested in what I was interested in, and he really wanted to get to know me and that felt good.

After a short while, I led him back down the path to the car and hated to let go of his hand when we reached the door, but he followed me over to the driver's side and opened my door for me.

Aw, a card-carrying member of the dying breed of gentlemen.

I sat down, started the car, and we jumped forward with a jerk. I took him on the tour of the neighborhood I grew up in, including the elementary school, high school, library, and community pool. I asked him questions about his life and he asked about mine. A friend once told me a first date is basically an interview, and I seemed to believe her at this point. I guess I hadn't really ever been on a first date before. Aaron and I were friends before we started dating and knew a lot about each other before the first "date" we ever went on alone.

Soon, I parked the car at the community baseball fields. The sun had set and the light of the moon was all that illuminated our walkway. He took my hand again, and I led him down a grassy path that was parallel with the train tracks. We walked hand in hand, talking until it was time to cross the tracks. We walked carefully passed over the tracks by some tall trees and then walked down a very steep, deep pathway out to a flat rock cliff.

The surface of the cliff was illuminated by the silvery-blue moon shining down from the sky. I led Nolan to the end of the cliff, and we looked down to the rocky beach below. I could feel him shaking as he realized it was easily more than one hundred feet down to the rocky beach below us. I giggled underneath my breath at his fear and backed us up a few feet to sit down on a boulder securely resting on the top of the rocky ledge.

Another breathtaking view of the river stood before us. A glance to our right showed the docks where the *Bailey* and the other boats were sleeping quietly for the night. We were right on a bend in the river so a look in front of us showed the point where the Ducks entered the water at Echo Point, and further down, we could see the baby grand piano—a rock formation that truly looked like a piano that had been tipped off a rock cliff and landed on its side. The Wisconsin River looked much more mysterious and magnificent by moonlight. The water was as still as glass, and a thousand shining stars reflected off its surface from above. Nolan slid his hand around my waist and pulled my hip in close to his.

"You were right. I could see this a million times over and never grow tired of it." Nolan turned to face me, and I looked up into his eyes. He carefully and gently brushed a tiny bit of brown hair from my eyes and tucked it behind my ear. Then he took my chin in his hand and sweetly pulled it ever so slightly upward until his lips barely brushed mine. An electrifying tingle shot down my face and through my entire body as I surrendered to his touch. He kissed me again but this time with more meaning, and I felt like I was floating on a fluffy, white cloud.

Nolan pulled back slightly and whispered, "I guess this is Make Out Rock?"

I giggled and replied, "Yeah. You can't help but fall to its power." My perma-smile was back, and I knew this was going to be the best summer of my life.

Chapter Seven

The next morning I said hi to Rob at the dispatch booth and took the long staircase down to the docks. Jack was already there, checking the oil on the *Bailey*.

"Hey kiddo!" he greeted me when I stepped on the back deck. "You ready for another fun-filled day on the Wisconsin River?" He was a little too chipper for this early in the morning.

"Are you drunk again?" I asked him, checking his eyes for a sign.

He laughed a big belly laugh and said, "No! I told you I would never do that again! Maybe I'm just in a good mood. Is that a crime?" He smiled at me, but I knew something was up.

Jack and I headed inside to start up the Bailey and check our tour book supply and prep the boat for the day. As soon as Jack turned on the two-way radio, it buzzed to life: "*General Bailey*, Dispatch." It was Rob up in the dispatch booth. Jack picked up the mouthpiece and said, "Go ahead."

"We've got Badgerland Tours coming in five minutes. Jack, will you be ready for early loading?"

"10-4, absolutely," he replied happily. Then he turned to me, "An OLS? Hot damn!"

Cha-ching!

An Old Lady Special (commonly called OLS by boat employees) was a jackpot!

Occasionally, a whole coach bus full of elderly ladies on tour through Wisconsin would stop at the Boats. Although it was sometimes a pain to load them all up, they were usually the most courteous and inquisitive passengers, and the best part was that each little old lady needed a guidebook to take home and show their grandchildren.

"Sweet! We haven't had an OLS yet this summer!" I said, while doing a very immature move that looked like a cross between an Irish jig and the potty dance.

"This is perfect timing. It's been so slow this summer, and my truck needs new rotors and brakes. I'm in some desperate need of some cold, hard cash." He paused and then turned to look me straight in the eyes. "Don't ever get married, Ava, because inevitably, your spouse will decide to have a sleepover with someone hotter than you in your own bed, and divorce is brutal on the checkbook."

I was in shock. I'd had no idea what had happened in the divorce other than it was messy, and poor Jack was left heartbroken. I didn't really know what to say, so we found ourselves in silence for a few moments.

I knew I hadn't sold many books so far this summer, but I didn't think it was my fault at all. It was plain math—more passengers equal more money. I gave the best tour I could each and every time I went downriver. I wasn't only motivated by money, I truly enjoyed what I was doing, and I'm the kind of person who does everything with my whole heart invested. I owed this trip to Jack, and I even considered giving all the profits to him and his truck.

After we quickly swept and cleaned up the boat, we were ready for loading. I noticed Jack was whistling an upbeat tune. I don't think I had ever heard Jack whistling before. We took our posts at the end of the dock and watched as a line of probably eighty-five elderly ladies was herded very slowly down the stairs. There was a younger woman, probably in her early thirties, with the group. She was clearly the ringleader, as she knew many of the ladies by name and escorted a few by herself down the stairs. Poor old Rob had to make multiple trips up and down the ramp pushing wheelchairs full of passengers. Following up the group was an overweight middle-aged man wearing navy blue head to toe—no doubt the bus driver.

We were in the best mood as the nice old ladies very carefully and slowly embarked onto the *Bailey*. I offered my hand many times to help some bridge the gap between the dock and the back deck of the boat. But as Jack and Rob were hoisting a wheelchair-bound passenger onto the boat, another lady wedged her bright white orthopedic shoes right in the gap between two of the stairs leading to the top deck. It took Jack and me many minutes to pry it free while she screeched, "Watch my bunions!" at us. Even so, I turned on the sweetness as I buttered up those old ladies, ready to graciously accept their dollar bills at the end of the tour.

Once the group had been loaded and all were successfully seated, the crew was ready to depart. As Jack pulled the boat away from the dock and turned our beauty around, he began to give the ladies a wonderful welcome. Before I knew it, someone yelled, "We can't hear!" and pointed to her ears. I smiled, nodded and bent down to turn up the sound system hidden underneath the guide's counter. When I popped back up, someone else yelled, "Where's the bathroom?"

What? No raising of hands? No polite, "Excuse me ma'am?" This seemed to be a rare breed of OLS. They were going to make me work for their money.

So I did work really hard, giving interesting and clear commentary, singing perfectly on every note, using downtime to engage in small talk with the ladies in the front row, and doing personal favors like opening and closing windows upon their request. It was one of my best tours in quite a while.

Thirty minutes later we were headed back upriver, which meant it was time for me to pass out the guide books so the passengers could look at them and decide if they wanted to purchase one. As I was gliding through the rows, I looked up and noticed we were passing a Duck. It was my oldest friend, Ted. He saw my OLS and gave me an enthusiastic thumbs-up. I think I saw him mouth, "Yeah, baby!" I replied with a thumbs-up and an obnoxious smile of my own. Then he gave me the phone sign and mouthed, "Call me later." I hadn't talked to Ted for a few months. I guess it was about time.

I returned back to my station in the front of the boat next to Jack. Traditionally, the driver gave the sales pitch. The pitch was carefully designed to brainwash the passengers into buying a guidebook. The driver would explain how wonderful the guidebooks were by carefully pointing out certain pictures inside. He'd comment on how useful it was to have a postcard for each picture from your trip, and then, for the frosting on the cake, he would pour on a little guilt explaining that your wonderful tour guide made a small portion of the sales from these books. Purchasing a book would be a wonderful way to thank your guide for the excellent tour she has provided for you.

When Jack was done, I decided to press my luck a little more by turning on some relaxing music from my iPod. Floating upriver surrounded by amazing scenery and listening to a beautiful song was like magic. These old ladies wouldn't know what hit them.

It was time to go collect my fortune. Jack said, "Good luck, kid," and I gave him a nod and a playful punch on the shoulder. I quickly walked past the first few rows and sped all the way to the back row of the bottom deck. A little tour guide trick is to start selling from the back row and move to the front. That way, the tourists can't see what others are doing. If you began in the front and the first few passengers decided to pass on the book, all the others seemed to think they would pass as well. And it would catch on like wildfire.

I leaned into the lady by the window in the back row, by putting on my sweetest tour guide voice and asking her if she'd like to purchase a book. She smiled at me and handed it back. No problem. I've never had one hundred percent of a boat buy. The next lady handed the book back to me as well, and then the next. And the next.

This was...interesting.

I continued through the rows. Old lady after old lady handed me their book back. I made it through the entire bottom deck without selling one single book. *Impossible.* I thought for a second that I should ask Jack to give the pitch again. Maybe these blue-hairs didn't have their hearing aids turned on. During the tour I had made an effort to speak with the ladies up on the top deck; perhaps I should have made an effort down here too.

The ladies on the back deck handed me the books, complaining that they couldn't hear me over the noise from the engines. I apologized and headed up the stairs to the top deck. The top deck, in general, was a pretty sweet ride. It was simply magical taking an open-air ride through the Dells with nothing to block your view. But as I should have guessed, row after row, the old ladies handed me their books back. Some said things like, "No thanks, but I really enjoyed your tour, young lady," or, "Your singing was beautiful, honey, but no thanks." I finished collecting the books and had not a single dollar in my hand.

What the hell?

I stormed through the top deck, down the stairs, opened the closet in the back where I kept the books, and threw them down haphazardly into the box. I was pissed. It felt as though row after row, each little old grandma stood up and smacked my cheek with as much force as her flabby arm could administer. A tear grew in my eye, and then I heard that sweet song still singing through the speakers. I left the closet, stormed up the aisle between all the empty-handed old ladies, slammed myself into my chair, and stopped my iPod mid-track.

"What the hell happened?" Jack loudly whispered at me.

"We got gotched." My arms were folded across my chest, breathing heavily. I picked up my yellow notebook and scratched a zero in for the trip. I threw it back on the counter without a care and let the pen roll off and drop to the floor.

"No shit?" Jack was baffled. I could see it in his face. Then he muttered, "Impossible," and hit the throttle. The faster we got back to the dock, the better.

After the gotch disaster, we hung our heads and headed up to the ticket booth looking for some jokes and funny stories from Suzanne. Brian was there, but no Suzanne.

"Hey, kids! So I heard your OLS gotched ya! That takes talent, seriously."

Boy, news travels fast. But how did anybody know?

Brian turned his back to the ticket window and held up a hand for a high five. We both completely ignored him.

Jack slammed his hand down on the ticket counter. "Come on! We just got off the dock! Who told you?"

I wanted to yell, "Amen!" but kept it to myself.

"Easy, Captain Jack. Rob watched the whole lot walk by the dispatch booth empty-handed and took a wild guess. He immediately called me up front to check as they shuffled by with their walkers and wheelchairs. I confirmed, not a single tour book in any hands!" He let out a laugh, annoying to only Jack and me, and we turned to leave the booth in frustration. Suzanne arrived for work at that same moment and blocked the door to the booth.

"Well, if it isn't the only crew ever to get gotched on an OLS!" There was that big, annoying laugh of hers again.

"Unbelievable," Jack muttered. "Let's get out of here, Ava." Jack pushed his way past Suzanne as she set her briefcase on the counter and opened the till. I followed him out the door, and we both could hear Suzanne and Brian still laughing as we headed back toward the docks.

The Lower Dells docks were located at the busy intersection of Highways 12 and 16. The corner lot contained a large Mexican restaurant that wasn't very tasty, a few shops with tourist junk (as Jack liked to call it), and an ice cream shop connected to the Last Chance. All of these were housed in two very long and awkwardly shaped buildings with siding painted in alternating barn red and sunflower yellow. If the intention was to attract visitors, they certainly did, but maybe not for the right reasons. In between those two oblong-shaped buildings was a courtyard of sorts with a seating area and planters. Tourists waiting for their boat to be loaded would lounge around here. It certainly did have a spectacular view of the Lower Dells docks and the Kilbourn hydroelectric power dam. Jack and I took a seat on a red bench and looked dejectedly out over the dock.

We sat in silence as I wondered where Nolan was. I knew he wasn't at Lower One. I took a quick glance to the left of the waiting area over towards Lower Two. It was another triangle booth, much smaller than Lower One, located at the end of the Mexican restaurant. It normally opened later in the day than Lower One, and no one was in there yet. I let out a sharp sigh—I wanted to see his handsome face. I knew that was the only thing that could cheer me up.

I screamed as I felt a quick and intense pain behind my left ear.

"You okay?" Jack asked, startled by my outburst.

I rubbed the area with my palm, and the pain slowly subsided. "Yeah, I guess." The pain diminished even more. "I've been getting these weird pains behind my eyes lately. I have no idea why."

"Huh," was all he could say. He stared off into the scene before us, breathing deeply. Neither of us had anything to say. I couldn't imagine my day going any worse. I was glad it was almost over. Then I had an idea.

"You know what?" I asked as I pulled out my phone. "Now's as good a time as any." I opened up UWSP's grade book and logged in.

"Good grief, you still haven't done that?"

"Nope." I clicked on the last semester and read the grades aloud. "Just as I suspected—two D's, two F's, and an A."

"An A? Congrats!"

"In choir," I explained.

"Holly hell. What a semester."

"I'm screwed."

We both took a deep breath and released it loudly. The silence continued a bit longer until a familiar system of alarms rang out in the distance, indicating one of the dam's gates was being opened. We watched gallons upon gallons of water pour through the concrete opening. Sometimes, when many of the gates were opened, the force of the water would churn up the minerals in the river and mix them with air. Fluffy, brown foam would build up and collect around the docks to create a topping that looked not unlike the top of a glass of freshly poured root beer.

Perhaps the sight reminded him of the head on a beer. "You really oughta hit the bar with me tonight, kid." He looked over at me with pleading eyes. I knew he was just looking for a friend.

Although I could see him from the corner of my eye, I didn't shift my focus from the dam. "I'm nineteen years old, Jack."

He looked back over the water. "Yeah, yeah, kid. I know."

Chapter Eight

When I got home that day I tried to put my bad grades out of my head and went straight up to my room to call Ted. I took a seat on my bed and then lay back on the pillow.

Ted answered the phone exclaiming, "Well, if it isn't good ol' Ava! Long time no talk there, sweetie! How's life treating ya?"

Ted was an adorably short, dark-haired, hilarious guy who rarely had a bad day and could make anyone laugh with a lift of one eyebrow. Although we tried to keep in touch when we went off to college, I hadn't talked to Ted for a few months. We had been good friends since we played blocks together in preschool, and although he and Aaron were best friends in high school, I still remained friends with Ted even after Aaron and I broke up.

"Hey, you wanna go get some ice cream and catch up? I'm sure you've got a little extra cash in your pocket after that OLS I saw you with this morning."

Oh God. Did he have to bring that up?

What I really wanted to do was call Nolan, but I knew I should remain loyal to my oldest friend and spend a little time catching up with him. After all, Ted was always good for a few chuckles. "Yeah, sure. That sounds great, Ted. Besides, I'm sure you've got a lot to tell me about your last semester in Milwaukee."

After I hung up the phone, I stood up off the bed, threw on a pair of jeans and a worn-out Milwaukee Brewers T-shirt, and tied my hair back into a ponytail. Before I went downstairs to tell my parents I was heading out, I couldn't resist taking a peek out the front window in my parents' bedroom at Animal Island across the street. My heart dropped when I didn't see a soul. I realized I wanted to see Nolan more than anything. Just one glance.

But as I was about to turn away, I noticed a shiny black car with dark windows pull up into the driveway of Animal Island and park. Two men wearing sunglasses and dark suits got out and casually looked around. They seemed terribly out of place, and I couldn't imagine why they would be at the employee housing. I watched in awe for a few more moments as they walked around to the white, two-story house at the end of the lot and knocked on the door. My watch bumped the windowsill as I tried to get closer, and it reminded me that I had to get going if I was going to pick up Ted.

I hopped in the Olds and headed north on Capital Street. Ted's family and my family both lived on the same street, only several blocks away from each other. The main drag, Broadway, cut Capital Street in half, and the strange thing was that on my side of Broadway all the street signs were spelled "Capital," and on his side they were spelled "Capitol." We both claimed our side was the correct spelling, but of course, neither way was ever proved to be right or wrong.

When I pulled up to his house, Ted popped out of the front door with his black and white cat, Mr. Kitty, prancing behind him. He turned around right before he got to his car and bellowed for Mr. Kitty to get back in the house. I leaned over the passenger side seat and yelled out the window, “Aw, come on! No cat for our ice cream run?” I laughed as Ted pulled open the door and then hopped into the passenger seat.

“Hey there, hot stuff! It’s so great to see you.” He leaned over and gave me a hug. My relationship with Ted had always remained platonic, although I thought for a while before I dated Aaron he might have wanted it to be more. I never felt that way about Ted and made sure he knew it. It actually was really nice to have a good guy friend. Sometimes I only wanted to get away from girl drama and have a friend who didn’t care about all that junk.

I parked the car in the Upper Dells parking lot, and we walked down the short hill to the Dairy Queen on Broadway. I don’t know why I hadn’t thought of it before, but at the bottom of the hill, before the Dairy Queen, was a DBT ticket booth.

“So, can’t stay away, huh?” Nolan was leaning out the window with the biggest smile on his face. His eyelashes seemed to be waving me closer. Visions of Make Out Rock filled my head. Butterflies instantly fluttered in my stomach, and soon, the whole world around us seemed to fade to a blissful blur. It was only me and him alone at the ticket booth. I felt my cheeks become rosy, and I was at a loss for words.

I had forgotten Ted was there until he cleared his throat, obviously uncomfortable, and brought the world zooming back into focus. I was about to introduce Ted when he said, "Hey, Nolan."

Wait. "Hey, Nolan?"

"Oh, hey there, Ted. I see you got back on the river today. Lucky guy."

They knew each other? How could this be possible?

"You two know each other?"

Ted jumped in, "Yeah, we met while I was driving the Ducks shuttle this morning."

It was entirely plausible that they met here. I wondered if they talked about me. Then I realized there was a potential problem—Aaron had probably told Ted about Nolan interceding at my house. Ted probably hated Nolan already.

An awkward silence followed, so I said, "We were just about to get some ice cream at Dairy Queen. Can I get you something?"

Nolan politely declined, and mentioned that he would be working at Lower Two tomorrow, and that I should stop by between trips. He gave me a smile that I knew was only for me, and his calm, charming eyes tried to give me a message that made me blush even more. I wasn't moving, so Ted grabbed my elbow and pulled me along. "Come on, Ava. See you later, man."

"See you tomorrow." I left the booth, but I could feel his eyes following me as I walked away.

When we got closer to the Dairy Queen window, Ted turned to me with a serious glare, and I knew I was in trouble. "Well, Ava, you have got a lot of explaining to do!"

I tried to play innocent. "What do you mean?" But I knew he could see right through me.

"I haven't seen you with that look on your face since Aaron finally started paying attention to you junior year! You are in trouble. This guy's got you all wrapped up already."

I knew he was right, but was too proud to admit it.

"I hate to be the one in the middle, but Aaron told me he thought you two were getting back together. Well, until some dude came out of nowhere and took a swing at him."

I looked down at the ground. "That dude was Nolan."

"Seriously? I knew I was getting a bad vibe from him."

"Hold on, you only have half the story. Aaron was practically forcing himself on me!"

"Really? I don't know..."

Ted was simply being overprotective. I was, after all, one of his oldest friends, and he saw what happened to me after Aaron broke my heart. I was able to change the subject while we were eating our cones by asking lots of questions about his adventures going to college in Milwaukee. I also tried to avoid talking about my crappy year at Stevens Point by only vaguely answering his questions, but he wasn't buying it. He could tell I was holding back, and I ended up spilling the beans about being somewhat depressed most of the year, and how my grades had suffered considerably.

"Dang! Two F's and Two D's?" He patted me on the back when all the color drained from my face. "Listen, Ava, you are a smart, determined woman with great plans for the future. You will figure this all out. You just have a little adjusting to do, and if I know you, you'll find your place in time."

"Thanks, Ted. That's awfully sweet of you." Somehow I had trouble believing him, however. We updated each other on our families, and he politely told me what he knew about what Aaron had been up to lately.

When I could feel the evening was about to end, I knew I had to confide in Ted. "Listen, could I ask a favor of you? Could you not mention to Aaron that I'm seeing Nolan? I don't really know what he was thinking the other day, and I just don't want to see another fight between the two of them."

Ted was a good friend, and I knew he would keep my secret. "Fine. But you have to promise me something."

"Sure, anything."

"Just keep me filled in on what's happening with Nolan. I just don't know about him, okay?" He looked up at me with pleading eyes. It was actually a bit startling.

What was he seeing that I wasn't?

"Don't you worry about me, Ted." I patted his shoulder.

"Just promise."

"Fine. I promise." I needed to change the subject quickly. "Hey, you wanna hit the go-kart track? You know, for old time's sake?" Ted and I frequented the go-kart track growing up, and I thought it might be a nice nostalgic plan for the rest of the night.

Ted gave me a big smile. “Absolutely.”

We finished our cones and then headed back toward the parking lot. By the time we walked by the booth again, it had closed up. I wondered what Nolan was doing at that exact moment.

Chapter Nine

Nolan worked at Lower Two the next day. I visited him a few times between trips but was sure to leave a little space for him to wonder about me. I also decided to spend a few breaks up at Lower One talking to Suzanne and Brian. The conversation turned serious early in the day when they started talking about Nolan.

"Well, I think he's a really nice guy," Brian was commenting. "He just oozes charm and really seems to have a good head on his shoulders."

"Oh, come on, Brian! Are you seriously getting sucked into his tractor beam? I can see right through that guy. He is as fake as fake can be." Suzanne was sitting in the ticket window, doodling on a pad of paper.

Brian challenged Suzanne. "The kid is like twenty years old! What do you think he's hiding?" Brian was leaning one elbow on the counter and looked very relaxed.

"Listen, I like the guy. He's a blast to work with here in the booth, but I'll be damned if there isn't something he's hiding from us." She tapped her pen on the glass counter and stared off into space, thinking. "He sure does have a fancy car and phone for a guy who works off of commission."

"Maybe his family has money. Have you ever asked him about his family?" Brian was pointing a finger in Suzanne's face.

Suzanne playfully slapped his finger down and said, "I don't know why you are getting so defensive! I said I like the kid. I'm just saying there is something about him that doesn't rub me the right way." Then she stared off into space again and said, "Let's see...armed robbery?... Oh! Drug lord?... Wait! I know, I know! Gang fighting..." That one made Brian laugh, although Suzanne was serious.

"There is no way that Nolan is into gang fighting! Give it up, Suzanne, maybe he's just a good guy."

They seemed to have forgotten I was sitting in the corner of the booth. I'm sure they wouldn't have had such a conversation if they remembered I was right there. I decided to give them a reminder and cleared my throat.

Brian turned toward me, and his face lit up like a Vegas hotel sign. "Oh, shoot! I forgot! Nolan is going to kill me!"

What?

Suzanne threw the pen at the ceiling, and it bounced off, landing on my lap. "Oh, see? I knew it. He's into murder!"

Brian shot Suzanne an angry look before turning back to me. "Go out to your car right now."

Suzanne was yelling now, "Don't do it! He manufactures homemade bombs!"

Although my heart rate sped up, I sat still and stared at them. Was Brian out of his mind?

"Come on! I promise you'll be happy. Just go out to your car and take a look." But I couldn't move. He walked a few steps closer to me and looked me dead in the eyes. "Seriously. Have I ever led you wrong before?"

No. Hadn't I known Brian as a good judge of character and a level-headed guy? So I slowly and anxiously slid off the stool and walked out of the ticket booth. I kept my eyes on Brian and Suzanne, not quite sure what to expect.

A Dells Boat tour bus filled with passengers from the Upper Dells crossed my path. I surveyed the parking lot but didn't see anything to be alarmed about. After all, I didn't quite know what I was looking for, and my imagination was definitely taking the better of me.

As I approached my Olds, I noticed something on my windshield. It looked like an envelope and some type of bundle wrapped in plastic. As I cautiously walked closer, I found a dozen red roses placed carefully under the left windshield wiper. They must have been beautiful many hours ago, but now they were dead and wilted from the summer sun. I laughed a little—they had dried and stuck to the windshield, and as I tried to pry them free, several of the petals fell to the ground and the stems broke.

The envelope was addressed to "My singing tour guide." A smile slowly crept onto my lips. Inside was a blank card with writing on the back.

Dear Ava,

Thank you for the amazing date the other day. I couldn't have imagined a better time. Your sweet smile is stuck in my mind, and I just have to get another fix. I would be honored if you would accept another date with me. Meet me at the Island at 8pm tonight.

Nolan

The huge smile on my face could not be hidden. I looked back at Lower One and saw Suzanne leaning far out of the booth window watching me. I chuckled to myself—how could I have let her scare me? I didn't care what anyone said; I was intrigued and had to make my own decision. I was going to accept the ugly, wilted roses and go on that date. I only had to make it through the day, first.

I looked out toward the dam. From the spot where my car was parked I could see the dock where Jack was loading up the passengers for our next tour. "Crap!" I yelled and sprinted past Lower One.

I could faintly hear Suzanne yelling, "What's the matter, kid? A swarm of bees fly up your shorts?" followed by that familiar boisterous cackle. I just kept on running, all the way down to the boat.

Jack was already at the wheel, engines on, ready to pull away from the dock. I untied the bowline and mouthed "sorry" to him. He flashed a somewhat fake smile at me, and I quickly walked to the back of the boat, untied the stern, and gave us a push as we left. I walked through the crowd on the lower deck and approached Jack at the wheel.

He smiled more genuinely this time. "Glad you could make it, kid."

Jack picked up the microphone and turned on his tour guide voice. "Good morning, ladies and gentlemen, and welcome aboard the *General Bailey*. My name is Captain Jack, and I will be skillfully driving you down the Wisconsin River today. We have just embarked on a one-hour tour of the Lower Dells. Be ready to see some gorgeous rocky scenery, learn about the history and geology of the Dells, and hear Native American legends. Here to dazzle you with her verbal dexterity is your very punctual and talented tour guide, Ava!"

It was nearing the end of June and our full boat was an indication that tourism was finally starting to pick up. Another clear sign was that our trips were going well that day. We had sold considerably more guidebooks so far than the amount we had sold on any other given day that summer. I felt right at peace, doing what I was good at and making some money doing it.

Late in the tour, I was up on the top deck giving my spiel on the loggers that used to come down the river riding on rafts made from 100-foot-tall tree trunks tied together. It was another bright, sunny afternoon in Dells country, and Jack and I were both in a great mood.

We were coming up on a green army Duck and I knew instantly from the name on its side that it was Aaron's. I started explaining the next rock formation, Pulpit Rock, when we caught up to him. I waved politely and he put his thumb and pinkie up to his ear and mouth, giving the "call me" sign. I shook my head no and he mouthed "please" as I finished my spiel.

Jack hit the throttle and left the little Duck bobbing in our wake.

Just then I noticed Jack had propped open the windows above the dash so he could catch some breeze while he drove the boat. I looked down and the window seemed to have some sort of paper stuck to the underside of it. It even seemed to have writing on it. Could Jack be trying to send me a message? Sometimes he would tug on the microphone cord to indicate I had missed a cue or was repeating something I'd already said, but I'd never seen him use this technique before. I moved to the edge of the boat and leaned against the guide wires so that I could get a closer look at the writing. It said, *Whatever you do, do NOT come down*!

Do not come down? Why not? Was there an evil man in a ski mask holding him hostage at gunpoint? Was there a hole in the boat and we were slowly sinking? Just when I was about to panic and go down anyway, he pulled that piece of paper off and posted another. I read it through the glass: *I farted and it really stinks.*

I burst out laughing and heard Jack reciprocate downstairs. I realized he was throwing the boat in reverse to try to fight the current and stay positioned next to a sign on the wall posted by the US Geological Survey. It was time for me to continue my tour. Bursts of laughter were still sneaking up my throat, but I tried my best to force them back down. I would not let Jack get the best of me. I pushed my laughter deep into my belly and put on a very serious face. I lifted the microphone to my mouth and began talking, but every time I thought about Captain Jack sitting in his own stink, it made me giggle a little bit.

Chapter Ten

Jack and I unloaded our last boat and watched the passengers walk down the dock and out of sight. It was 6:15 and we were both beat. We walked down into the bottom part of the boat and Jack began to sweep the deck.

I totaled the day's sales after our six tours and cut Jack half of the profits. "Well, partner, we were one hundred twenty-five for six today! Here's ninety-seven bucks for you!" He took it with a smile, did a little bow, and said, "Thank you, ma'am. Now that's more like it."

We locked the Bailey to the dock and then headed out to the parking lot together. Jack seemed awkward, like he had something to tell me but didn't know how to say it.

He was looking down at his feet when he said, "I know you've noticed my unexplainable good mood lately. Well...I met someone." I looked up at his face and saw a wide smile stretched across it. "She's perfect for me." He stopped at the back bumper of his truck, turned, and looked right into my eyes. "I've just never felt quite this way before."

"Jack...that's great! Really, I'm just so happy for you." I hoped this lady was perfect for him and that Jack could find the peace in his heart that he deserved. I put my right arm across his upper back and gave his shoulders a squeeze. He smiled at me, said, "See you tomorrow," and got in his truck.

I turned and opened my car door and saw a shadow on my car. Someone was behind me.

"I hear you're dating someone," a familiar voice said.

I took a deep breath and turned around slowly. "It's over between us, Aaron," I said firmly. "I've told you that already."

He took a step closer to me and I flinched, thinking about the last time we were this close. Where was Nolan? Would he pop out of the bushes and come to my rescue?

"Ava, I need you."

I tried, but couldn't keep fear from my face.

There was the popping sound of a car door opening and Jack get out of his truck. "Is there a problem, here?"

Aaron's tone changed. "Oh, hey Jack. No, no problem here. I was just saying hello."

"Ava, go on and head home," Jack told me.

"Thanks, Jack." I felt brave with Jack standing there, so before I left, I looked deep into Aaron's eyes and said gently, "I'm letting you go, Aaron. She's out there somewhere, waiting for you. But it's not me."

Aaron looked annoyed. "Yeah, whatever."

I got in my car and pulled away. Jack was talking with Aaron as I left the Lower Dells parking lot. I hoped he could smooth things over with Aaron and talk him into leaving me alone. As I passed Lower One I thought about Nolan. I was supposed to meet him at Animal Island in an hour and a half!

A sudden nervousness swept over me. What was I going to wear? Where would he take me? My brain was swimming with questions, and the next thing I knew I was at my front door, and I barely remembered driving home.

My mom and dad were talking on the front porch. They were each holding a small glass of red wine and discussing something quietly. They looked very serious and even concerned, but unlike the squabble from the other night, they seemed to be on the same side this time. Dad reached over and patted Mom's knee right as they noticed me standing before them.

"Everything okay, honey?" Mom asked. "You have a strange look on your face."

"Absolutely. Everything okay with you two?"

"You bet. Just enjoying the evening sunset."

"Okay. I'm gonna go take a shower."

I supposed I could be making something out of nothing, so I smiled and went inside. Laura was sitting at the kitchen table, and since I hadn't seen her for a long time, I stopped to chat before I got ready for my date.

"Hello there, stranger!" she said. "Tell me, how is it that our schedules have been exactly opposite all summer long? We live in the same house, but I never ever see you!"

"I know, sis. It's crazy." I took a chip from the bag lying on the table. "So how are things on the Upper?"

"You know, same as things on the Lower, I'd assume. I've been driving a bit on trips, but they won't let me dock yet." Then something popped in her head quickly. Laura had a short attention span and was easily distracted. "Oh my God! I totally forgot to tell you! The other day, I was carrying a brand-spanking new box of a hundred fifty guidebooks down from the office, and my sunglasses slipped off my head, so I bent over to pick them up, and my foot was right on the middle of where the two docks met and my ankle twisted and...BOOM!" She jumped off her chair for effect and I was so startled I bit my tongue. She was acting the whole thing out now. "I dropped the whole damn box into the river!"

"Oh my God! That's like two hundred bucks down the drain!" I tasted blood in my mouth.

"Yeah, I know!" She was bouncing, all excited from her story. "And right when the box went out of sight, I hear some guys sitting over at the dispatch stand laughing their butts off! They totally saw it all! I had to go back up to the office to beg for another box! I don't think I'll ever live that one down."

My sister was always good for a laugh. I told her briefly about my upcoming date and then headed upstairs to shower and change. As I climbed the stairs my phone rang out—a new email. I swiped the screen and swallowed hard. It was from the Dean of Education at UW–Stevens Point.

My stomach dropped out, and my pulse quickened as I stopped, frozen in the middle of the staircase.

"No, no, no," I whined, terrified.

I jogged up the last few steps, my hands shaking and tears forming in my eyes. I entered my room and shut the door quickly, collapsing to my knees. I took a shaky breath and then read the email.

It was just as I dreaded. I would not be considered for the School of Education my sophomore year and, in addition, my bad grades had landed me on academic probation. I closed my eyes and dropped my head in my hands, defeated and angry.

It was all so real now. I screwed up. Fat tears began to fill my eyes, and my shoulders shook as I allowed myself to cry. How could I have done this? What would my parents think of me? A whole year of college tuition, wasted.

The tears flowed for several minutes as I felt sorry for myself. But then I heard the front door shut as my parents entered the house. I didn't want them to know about the email, at least not for now. I sucked in a deep, cleansing breath in an effort to clear my head.

I had a date to go on tonight. A date with someone who made me feel really happy. I showered and dressed, vowing to myself that I would deal with college later.

At 7:58, I said goodnight to my family, and headed out the front door. I glanced over at Animal Island and saw Nolan chatting with some Upper guides near the bonfire. The walk around the block was short, but by the time I arrived at the bonfire site, the guides had left, and Nolan was sipping from a water bottle, staring into the orange flames absent-mindedly.

As I approached, Nolan rose from his seat on the grass. He looked very stylish wearing a plain white polo and blue plaid golf shorts.

"You look amazing," he said quickly, but then added, "What's wrong?"

Uh-oh, it was written all over my face.

"Nothing, I'm fine." I pasted a smiled onto my lips.

Nolan held his hand out to me. "Come here."

I sat down next to him and stared into the fire. I would have to come clean.

He took the hand he was holding and lifted it to his lips, administering a gentle kiss. "Please, Ava. What's bothering you?"

I took a deep breath through my nose as I pulled out my cell phone, handing it to Nolan. I waited while he read.

"Oh. Jeez. I'm really sorry, Ava."

I felt the sting again and fought back a tear. *No, not now.*

"I've never wanted to be anything but a teacher," I sniffled. "I just don't know what to do."

Nolan slid his arms around my back and sweetly kissed the side of my face near my eye. Then he spoke quietly in my ear, only for me to hear. "Here's what you do. You chase your dream. You get back up and try harder. Look, you haven't been kicked out, you've only been warned. You've been given a second chance and you're gonna take it."

He was sweet. Picking me up when I was down. I smiled through my tears.

He kissed the side of my head this time and then pulled back slightly. "Ava, you're a great teacher. I've seen it in action. You can't give up now. Hundreds of future school children will miss out."

I laughed gently. "Thanks, Nolan." I turned my head to meet Nolan's eyes. They emanated sincere concern. My heart melted. He really cared about me.

"Anyway, I guess there's not much I can do about it now. I'll just have to really focus when school starts again in the fall."

Nolan caught the last tear with his thumb before it could drip down my cheek. "You're exactly right," he said.

I looked around. There were two cabins on the right side of the fire and four on the left. Each cabin had olive green siding and a red roof and was basically the size of my parents' living room. The large, two-story, white house stood on the corner of the lot. It looked like it had seen better days. There were a few old trees scattered throughout the lawn between the two rows of cabins, and there was a gravel driveway running up the left side of the property.

"Which one is yours?"

"Right here." He pointed to the second cabin on the right side. "You want the grand tour?" He stood up and offered a hand.

Two crooked and wooden steps stood in front of a ragged screen door. As he led me through the door, I noticed a jacket hanging from a bright blue boat cleat screwed into the wall. We took a sharp turn to the left and were instantly in the space used as the living room, dining room, and bedroom. A small, hunter green, obviously used loveseat was pushed up against the window in the front wall. At the window on the opposite wall was a twin bed. Behind the wall by the front door was a tiny three-piece bathroom, and on the other side of the wall hosting his bed was a kitchen just as tiny as the bathroom. The overall feeling was definitely old, but it was clean and smelled faintly like cologne I had smelled once before.

"I'm trying to read your face, but I can't tell what you're thinking. Is it that bad?" Nolan kicked a lone sock out of sight under the bed.

"No, no, it's very quaint. It's perfect for your summer home." I said sincerely. He smiled and leaned in to kiss me on the forehead, then moved his mouth deliciously close to my ear and whispered, "I've missed you."

Nolan grabbed my hands and interlaced our fingers, twisting our arms up so he could hold my hands close to his quickly beating heart. He kissed my forehead again, and then let go of my hands so he could wrap his arms around my waist. The gap between us slowly closed as he pulled me in until our bodies touched. He buried his face in my hair and took a deep breath. It sounded like he said, "Mmmmm," quietly, but I couldn't be sure. Nolan rubbed his hands across the top of my back. There was something so satisfying about being held by Nolan. I felt so safe, so comfortable.

I had missed him, too. But how could this be? I had only met the guy a few weeks ago, but somehow I felt like I had been dating him for several months.

The side of my head snuggled right up into his shoulder, and I gently closed my eyes, allowing the feelings of peace and happiness to fill my heart.

As if there was music playing in his head, Nolan began to sway us back and forth like we were slow dancing. It was very sweet and gentle...and then a gargle from my stomach broke the whole serenity of our dance.

He pulled away, raising an eyebrow at me.

"Sorry, that was my stomach," I smiled at him sheepishly. "I hope you had dinner plans for us."

"Of course I do." He grabbed his wallet and car keys off the table by his bed and led me by the hand out the door.

Outside his cabin was a silver car that looked very fast and very cool. I don't know how I missed it when we were outside before. Like the gentleman that I knew him to be, Nolan walked over to the passenger side door, unlocked it, and opened it for me. I slid onto a very comfortable beige leather seat. The fancy control panel caught my eye while Nolan shut my door and walked around to the driver's side. It had some type of sophisticated computer in the place where my Oldsmobile had only a radio. I gently moved my fingers over the dials and wondered where he got the money for such a fancy car. Nolan hadn't entered the car yet—he was standing outside his door texting someone. I hoped it was his mom and not some old girlfriend.

He finally pulled open the door and sat down. "It's no Cutlass, but I hope it'll do."

"Yes, I suppose I can handle it," I teased.

He set the keys on a spot near the console and then pushed a button that I could only assume was the ignition since the car hummed to life, and he smoothly pulled out of the driveway. I knew nothing about cars, but I was totally impressed.

"I say let's take your car whenever we go out." I moved my hand over the console and placed my palm on his arm.

"So you'd like to go out with me more?" He moved his arm so his hand could hold mine in his.

"I don't know what it is, but I feel very comfortable with you. I really enjoy your company." The cutest smile slid across his lips. "So where are we going?" I said, not taking my eyes off his.

Nolan took me out to one of my favorite restaurants—High Rock Cafe. A classmate of mine from high school had studied in culinary school, and then a friend and he were able to open a two-story restaurant in a prime location on Broadway in the downtown area of the Dells.

We had plenty of conversation at dinner exploring each other's history. He shared with me information about his family, high school experiences, and past relationships. I did the same, but left out most of the info about Aaron, especially the drama involved with that relationship. Besides, I had plenty of stories to share from high school. Almost three hours flashed by and we didn't even notice the restaurant had cleared out. Our waitress finally hinted that we'd have to leave soon since they were closing.

We decided to take a little walk around and check out some of the shops that lined the main drag downtown. A four-lane bridge crossed over the river near the power dam and then under the railroad bridge that was still in use. Taking this former bridge was the only way to get to the downtown shopping area. Following the road past the bridge in the opposite direction for a few miles would run you straight into the town of Lake Delton. Along this road, you could see all the major water parks, go-kart tracks, mini-golf courses, and about fifty hotels. This road wasn't very pedestrian friendly, though, so most of the shops and bars were in the downtown area on Broadway.

We walked all the way through the crowded sidewalks and down to the train bridge where we stopped to rest on a bench near the old Upper Dells dock building. This cream-colored, two-story building was original to the turn of the century when the boat tours were one of the few attractions in the Dells. It was big and beautiful and oozed tradition and history in my mind. I looked up at the humongous train bridge over our heads. "Did you know this bridge is the main reason the town of Wisconsin Dells was settled?"

"Once a tour guide, always a tour guide," Nolan teased. I gave him a playful slap on the leg, and he said, "Okay, okay, go on with it. I'd love to know some more Dells history!"

"In the mid-1800s, a town called Newport sat several miles down the river from this point. In 1855, construction of a new railroad from Milwaukee to La Crosse was being planned to pass through the little town. The people of Newport knew the railroad's passing would bring considerable wealth with new shops and factories. The men of Newport who owned land the railroad company desired jacked up their prices, looking to make a profit, but the railroad company saw through these men's high prices and decided to build the railroad upriver about three miles at this exact site we sit at today. Knowing that a railroad would bring them wealth, the people of Newport packed up their things and moved their town to the site of the railroad, leaving the city of Newport a ghost town almost overnight. Old newspaper articles say entire houses were moved over the frozen river, pulled by mules. All that's left of the lost city of Newport is a few stone pillars on the riverfront. Pretty cool, huh?"

"Interesting."

I was sure he was only humoring me. Did anyone besides me think this stuff was incredibly neat? I went on purely to torture him. If he humored me more, then perhaps he was a keeper.

"You're a very good teacher, you know. You make things that are boring sound interesting. I could sit here and listen to you all night long. I mean it!" He winked and put a hand on my knee. A pleasant chill ran down my spine. So he was either a keeper or very good at buttering me up.

"Well, I'd be happy to sit with you until 12:30. I know you are out on your own, but I have a curfew, you know."

"Ah yes, 12:30. Don't worry—I told you parents love me. Do you know why?"

"Um, because of your undeniable wit and charm?"

He didn't expect that and laughed adorably. "No! Although that does make a lot of sense. Parents love me because I'm always respectful of the curfew."

"Ah, the curfew. Right."

"You will be home not a tick past 12:30, young lady! What time is it now, anyway?" Nolan pulled his phone out of his pocket and pressed the button on the side. "Midnight already? Man, I'm going to hate to bring you back so soon." Then he leaned over and kissed the side of my head, right above my ear.

I felt the same way. I stood up from the bench and said, "Well, mister, we better get walking back to the car." He stood up and grabbed my hand in agreement. We happily walked hand in hand all the way back to the parking lot.

"What time do you have to work tomorrow?" I asked along the way.

"Tomorrow..." He was thinking. "I have tomorrow off. I almost forgot."

"You do? So do I, actually!" Come on, Nolan, take the hint. I wanted so badly to spend the whole day with him.

We had returned to his car and I leaned my lower back near the bumper, while Nolan stood in front of me. I looked up at the clear sky filled with tiny sparkling stars and a half moon shining down on us from space—another beautiful night in the Dells. Nolan surprised me by picking me up by the hips and setting me down on the trunk of his fancy car.

"Really...you have tomorrow off?" he asked. I let my knees fall out and invited him to fill in the space with his body. I rested my arms on his shoulders and he wrapped his arms behind my waist. "Do you have any plans with the family?"

"No. I have nothing planned for tomorrow." I ran my fingers through the hair on the back of his head. "Do you?" Our lips were almost touching, and I thought he was going to kiss me, but instead he said, "I do now. I'll pick you up in the morning around ten," and then he leaned in, gently rubbing his lips on mine. He reached up and stroked the side of my face with his warm hand. His body inched closer and closer until I could feel his broad chest on mine.

"Oh, Ava," he breathed. Then he wrapped his lips tightly around mine, knowing how to make me fall undone.

It was a good thing I was already sitting, or my legs may have given out on me. I let the kiss continue, but too soon my head fought with my heart. "I have to get back," I murmured through the kiss, not wanting to stop.

"One more minute," he whispered back, still kissing me sweetly.

I wanted to never stop. I wanted to stay right there in the parking lot under an umbrella of summer stars forever.

Oh, what this man does to me.

Chapter Eleven

The next morning I woke up early, the kiss replaying over and over in my head. I was anxious for the day's activities, although Nolan wouldn't tell me what we were doing, only to be ready by ten. I took a shower, cleaned up my bedroom, and then headed downstairs to see what my parents were up to.

My father had taken a day off from work and was reading what looked like a very old scrapbook. My mother was at the stove frying eggs. I sat down on the couch next to my dad.

"What are you reading?" I looked over at the book.

"Haven't I ever shown you this before? It's been on our shelf in the living room for ages, and now I'm just getting around to looking closely at it. It's a family document scrapbook. I'm interested in researching our family's history. Your grandfather spent much of his short life interviewing family members, reading family documents, and visiting graveyards to try to trace our roots back as far as he could. He collected the items in this book before he died. I'm trying to honor his memory and continue on his quest."

"That's really cool, Dad," I told him as he turned the pages.

"Your grandfather was able to go back one hundred years to your great-great grandfather Arthur Gardner. I figure with today's technology, I could go back another hundred!"

I watched as Dad turned the pages in the old book. I spotted a picture of a man and a woman holding a tiny baby in front of an old farmhouse.

"Who is that?"

"That'd be Edna and Arthur Gardner. Edna is holding your great-grandfather, Robert. They lived on the outskirts of the Dells in the early 1900s. I think Robert was born in the latter part of 1913."

I looked closer at the old black and white photo and noticed something in the window of the house. It looked like the blue rock I found a few years ago in the basement and is now sitting on the bookshelf in my bedroom. I always thought that rock was something my parents found on one of their vacations abroad, but now that I thought about it, both rocks looked an awfully lot like the strange blue rock I almost tumbled down the hill to gather.

My father noticed me studying the picture and interrupted my train of thought. "It was unusual for families to get their photo taken in front of their own homes. Most people had to go to the photographer's studio. In this case, H.H. Bennett was probably one of the only photographers in the Dells at the time, and his studio was downtown." He flipped the photo over to look for markings on the back but didn't find anything. Then he went back to studying the front of the picture, presumably looking for hints. "What's this in the window?"

"Oh, I think that's that blue rock. I've been wondering, Dad, what is the story on that?"

"Well, you know, I'm not exactly sure myself. Your mother and I found it in a box of junk at your Grandma's house several winters ago. She must have packed it up when we moved her into the nursing home and the box has sat all closed up in the cellar of our basement for many years. I took it because I remember looking at it as a kid. It was on the mantle above the fireplace for many years, until one day my mother took it down and boxed it up."

"I found it in our basement, and now it's up in my room on my bookshelf."

"It's in your room?" He looked startled, and I heard my mom drop a dish in the sink.

"Oh, sorry, Dad. I guess I should have asked first. Do you want me to put in back in the basement?"

"No, no. You won't be here much longer before you have to go back to school anyway." He went back to flipping through the book.

I wondered what that meant. Obviously the rock had sentimental value to my father. I had taken it up to college with me this past year, as a memento of home, but now I would have to remember to put it back in the basement instead of taking it with me back to school.

Back to school.

I hadn't mentioned my academic failures to my parents yet. I was legally an adult, and old enough to make my own decisions about my life, but somehow I still felt like a child under my parents' rule. They would be disappointed when I told them about my academic probation, that was for sure. Maybe they didn't have to know. At least not yet.

I looked over at my dad, still paging through the scrapbook and taking notes. I was so proud of my father. He was always a goal-orientated person and never a quitter. I was sure he wouldn't stop until he traced our family line at least a hundred years further than my grandfather had.

I couldn't quit, either. I had to do better next semester.

"Good luck, Dad." I said. "Let me know if I can do anything to help." I kissed him on the forehead and walked into the kitchen to say good morning to my mother.

"How was your date last night?" she asked.

"It was good, Mom. I really like Nolan." I picked up a piece of toast and began to butter it.

She poured a glass of orange juice and handed it to me. "Nolan seems like a very nice young man."

"Thanks, Mom. I think so too." I took a bite of toast, chewing for a few seconds before I continued. "I'm going to spend the day with him. You don't think it's too soon, do you?" I knew not a lot of people were able to have an open relationship with their mother, but I was happy that I felt comfortable talking with her about my love life.

"If it feels right, then it's not too soon." She took a drink of juice from her own cup. "You have a good head on your shoulders, Ava. I'm not at all concerned that you are jumping into anything before you are ready." She scooped up some eggs with her fork and poked them in the air at me. "But with that said, make sure you aren't jumping into anything before you are ready, if you know what I mean."

I knew exactly what she meant.

Later I sat on the couch in the front living room pretending to read the paper. I was really stealing glances out the front window at Animal Island. Nolan's car wasn't parked outside of his cabin. I wondered where he was and if the clock could move a bit faster so ten o'clock could roll around.

I tried to busy myself with the newspaper until I noticed Nolan's car pull up in front of the house. I jumped up, grabbed my bag, and yelled to my parents that I was heading out.

Nolan was out of the car and coming up the walkway when I met him. He kissed me quick on the lips and said "Good morning, beautiful."

"It was a long night without you," I said flirtatiously.

"I agree. But at least we have the whole day to spend with each other."

I smiled at him, and then he turned and we got inside the fancy silver car. "Where are we off to this morning?" I inquired while I buckled my seatbelt.

He pulsed his eyebrows but said nothing as we pulled away from my house and drove down Minnesota Avenue towards Oak Street. I was proud of Nolan for learning the local back roads so quickly. He'd be a true native in no time. But then a thought hit me.

"Hey, what's today's date?"

"It's June 30th, I think."

"Oh my gosh. I can't believe it's almost July! Do you have any plans for The Fourth? They usually take a boat out on the Upper Dells to watch the fireworks. Then they beach it and build a big bonfire for the rest of the night. It's a pretty cool party."

He smiled while keeping his eyes on the road but then said nothing for a few seconds, and I thought perhaps I had jumped the gun. Did he not want to plan something with me a few days into the future? A small panic stirred up in my stomach, until he said, "There is nothing I'd rather do that day than be by your side." He moved a hand over and placed it gently on my leg. The panic in my stomach was easily pushed aside as some lovely butterflies of excitement took over.

We had arrived on the top of a hill behind the popular Pirate's Cove mini-golf course. Within seconds I realized we weren't golfing and I could not control my excitement. My jaw dropped to the floor. "Oh my gosh! I've always wanted to do this!" How did he know?

We both got out of the car and met at the ticket booth. Nolan told the attendant, "Hi, I'm Nolan Hill. I called ahead."

I looked at the price chart and realized he was spending a pretty penny on me. I suddenly felt a little guilty and offered to pay for my own fifty-dollar ticket.

Nolan pushed my hand aside and said, "You simply are adorable, but absolutely not."

I couldn't argue with those eyes, so I quietly put my credit card back into my purse and waited patiently as he paid the hundred dollars with cash. Soon, a man in a pilot's shirt, much like the ones we wore to work at the boats, led us to the landing pad behind the booth. Sitting up on top of a small hill on a square of concrete was a helicopter. Its propellers were already in motion and the sound was so loud I covered my ears with my hands. I had always wanted to take a helicopter ride over the city but never got around to it, so I was very excited to take this trip and to be able to sit right next to Nolan while I experienced it!

They buckled us in tightly and handed us headphones with little microphones attached so we could communicate with each other while in the air.

We took off and flew east toward my parents' neighborhood. Instantly I realized Nolan was nervous. He had his eyes closed, taking deep breaths with his head leaning back against the headrest. Of course, he was afraid of heights. And yet he knew I would love this and took me up here anyway. What a sweetheart.

I grabbed his hand and squeezed tightly, placing my other hand on top. "Thank you," I whispered, not knowing if he could hear me through the microphone.

A few minutes into the trip I saw Nolan relax a little. I peered out the window and quickly found the railroad bridge and bustling Broadway. We flew over my elementary school, the Catholic church, post office, and community pool. We followed Minnesota Avenue past the library. Nolan pointed out his window saying he could see my house and Animal Island, so I leaned over, pressing into him as I looked. It was such a great new perspective from up above, seeing everything I was so familiar with in a completely different way. I could see my mom's vegetable garden that takes up the second lot adjacent to our house. I could see all the way down Capital Street to Ted's house. I thought for a moment I could even see Mr. Kitty lounging in the front lawn.

Then the pilot changed directions and headed down River Road until we met the river. Nolan spotted the place I had brought him on our first date and pulled me back over to his window. He kissed my forehead as we relived the magical night from a few days ago.

I imagined myself as an eagle stretching my wings and soaring over that handsome brown channel. The towering stone cliffs looked a little less impressive from above, but I still was amazed by the beauty of the sight. I noticed a tour boat making its way downriver, but couldn't quite tell which one it was from above. There were many tour Ducks, one after another, slowly swimming their way downriver, indicating great crowds for that attraction today. We finally made it back to the docks where I could see a tour boat being loaded. Tiny little heads made their way down the loading stairs and onto the dock. There were several gates open on the dam, and it was interesting to see the water rush in from above the dam through the gates and then crash down into the Lower Dells.

The helicopter tour ended more quickly than I wanted it to. We landed back on the hill, the crew unbuckled us, and we jumped down from the helicopter. We thanked our pilot, I gave him a tip, and then Nolan grabbed my hand and walked me over to a field behind the landing pad. On top of the hill, the view was almost as gorgeous as it was from the sky.

"That was amazing," he commented.

We stood looking over the Lower Dells docks. "I completely agree. It was so cool for me to see my town from up above. It was perfect. Thank you so much, Nolan."

"You're more than welcome."

I looked back over the city, but soon felt Nolan's stare on my face. "A penny for your thoughts?" I said.

"Oh, I was just wondering what I ever did to gain the attention of such a wonderful woman."

I think I blushed three shades of red.

"Anyway, are you ready for our next destination?"

"Absolutely!"

Nolan had sought Suzanne's advice on the best beaches on the river and she had raved about her favorite spot called Birchwood Beach on the Upper Dells. We drove down the scenic and winding River Road and parked in a gravel parking lot. To my surprise, he opened up the trunk and took out a blanket and picnic basket! We walked up a dirt pathway through a prairie bursting with wild flowers and into the woods. I had taken the pathway a few times with my sister before, but I had forgotten how long of a walk it was.

We walked holding hands and talked about our futures. He asked me why I wanted to be a teacher and what grade I wanted to teach. I spoke for a long time about the experiences I've had working with children and my hopes for the future. Even though it was painful, I felt comfortable enough confiding in him the challenges I suffered through last year.

"Ava, you know I think you are going to be an excellent teacher. You are so understanding, patient, and so easy to listen to. I know your students are going to love learning from you."

"Thank you." I squeezed his hand. "That really means a lot to me."

"And don't worry about your academic probation. Sometimes life hands us challenges, but overcoming them makes us feel that much more proud of our accomplishments."

I nodded my head and smiled sweetly at him. It sounded a bit cheesy, yes, but it was exactly what I needed to hear. He was right. Most of the summer I had wondered if I could actually become a teacher and Nolan seemed to believe that I could.

I realized I didn't know much about Nolan's plans for the next few years of his life, so I asked him what his hopes and dreams for his future were, but he seemed to not be as driven as I was. He mentioned wanting to go to college, but hadn't applied to any yet.

"But I thought you just graduated? Why didn't you choose a college yet?"

"I graduated a year ago but spent this last year helping my parents out in their online business. I want to go to college someday, but I'm just not sure I'm ready yet." Nolan looked down at the ground, and for the first time since I met him, I thought I spotted a hint of embarrassment in his face. I didn't quite understand what he meant by that comment. College is a time to grow and change and really explore who you want to be. How could someone not be ready for that?

As he continued, it soon became clear to me that he really wasn't sure what he wanted to do with his life yet. He was talking in circles, mentioning he wanted to study law or perhaps spend a year or two in Africa with the Peace Corps.

It was a definite turnoff. I always thought I'd end up with someone who was as driven and goal-oriented as I was in my life.

I decided to drop it for now. We were both young, and although I had known for many years what I wanted to do with my life, there were plenty of people who take many years to decide. Plus, I wasn't ready to break up with him today over his life choices. I craved the way he made me feel when I was with him. He was like a drug I wanted more and more of. Maybe I could lead him in the right direction later on.

We emerged from the forest and were standing on top of a steep hill. Right below us was a sandy beach void of any other humans. We scaled down the rocky pathway and found a spot in the sunshine to lay a blanket down. Nolan had packed a delicious lunch, complete with ham and cheese sandwiches, red grapes, Doritos, and my favorite soda, Fresca.

"This is wonderful!" I told him as he fed me a grape.

While we ate, we watched the waves roll into the beach, tourists drift by on their pontoons, and a group of drunk and very loud college kids float downriver in a chain of black inner tubes. Besides the distractions in front of us, our conversations continued and were meaningful and insightful all at once.

"Tell me more about your family. You said your dad was doing some research into your family's history?" Nolan seemed honestly interested, and I was happy to share.

I told him what I knew about the Gardners—that we have been living in the Dells for more than a hundred years and that most of each generation's males were farmers. "My father, in fact, was the first male in many generations that did not take up farming."

"Interesting. You know, you should be very grateful that your family has taken the time to collect those documents and pictures because my family doesn't know much at all about our history."

"Really? That's a shame. Maybe someday you could do your own family research." He nodded in agreement. "I was just looking at some old photos with my father and found a picture of a special rock from 100 years ago that my family still has! Can you believe that?"

"Really? That's so neat," he replied truthfully.

The sun was rising high in the sky and we were getting pretty hot so we decided to wade in the cool water. I walked out as far as I could until the water was up to my mid-thigh. The soft sand beneath my feet felt heavenly. I dipped my hands and arms into the water as well. "You should have told me to bring a suit. I love swimming!"

He was about to reply when an Upper Dells tour boat came cruising around the corner. I could recognize the voice of the guide in a heartbeat. It was Laura!

"Hey! It's my sister! Hi, Laura!" I jumped and yelled and waved from the shore.

Nolan joined me waving and screaming, "Hey!"

Laura noticed us over on the beach and we heard her announce, "Off to your right, you can see my big sister and her boyfriend enjoying this beautiful scenery. Let's all wave to them!"

My boyfriend? My heart skipped a beat. Yes. I guess he was my boyfriend.

I smiled as wide as the river until I realized what was about to happen. Laura's boat driver, Phil, gunned the throttle. "Back up!" I frantically yelled. The boat's wake was moving quickly towards us. We tried to shuffle back as fast as we could, but before we knew it, the wave splashed onto us, getting us wet up to our chests. We both stood there stunned and dripping as we heard Laura saying over the microphone, "Have fun, you two!" and then the boat headed off into The Narrows.

And then we could do nothing but laugh. We laughed for a full minute before I saw the playful danger in his eyes. He smiled as he moved closer to me, arms out.

"No! No!" I yelled, half screaming, half giggling. "Don't do it!" I backed up towards the safety of the beach, but I was too slow. Nolan picked me up and gently slammed us both down into the warm water. We laughed and splashed together in the warm river water. My tank top stuck to my skin and made a nice bathing suit, but his T-shirt was a little too baggy and bulky in the water. He took it off and threw it on the beach. The sight of his muscular body sent warm shivers down my spine. His chest was smooth and muscular, and before I could think of any ramifications, I traced it with my trembling fingers. I couldn't help myself. But I pulled my hand back quickly when I realized what I was doing and there were several seconds of awkwardness that followed.

I turned away when I felt my face begin to flush. "Follow me," I called cheerfully, and swam off toward the rocky cliffs.

Nolan followed me to the sandstone tower, and we stood in river water up to our waists touching the soft rock. It was pinkish and cream-colored and broke easily in our hands. A glance around the side of the wall revealed a small alcove beyond a huge fallen boulder. Nolan followed me as I swam around the side of the cliff, and then we scaled a slippery boulder to enter the cave-like opening. It was a rock room with tall stone walls on three sides of us and the fallen rock blocking the entrance. Tall pine trees above us created a canopy of privacy.

The water was deep in this little cave, and although I couldn't touch the bottom, Nolan could. He sweetly picked me up by my hips, and I stopped treading water to put my legs around his waist. I looked deep into his eyes as I wrapped my arms around his back. He said nothing, but slowly kissed my lips. Soon the pace picked up, sending my heart beating wildly, and lighting a fire somewhere below my waist. He kissed me differently than I'd experienced with him before, caressing my hair and shoulders with his fingertips as the waves entering the cave bobbed us up and down in the soft water. It was our own little, incredibly romantic world. A small ray of sunshine had broken through the canopy of trees above us and shone down upon our heads as we kissed, the water sparkling around our wet bodies.

"You're so beautiful," Nolan whispered as he kissed my cheek with tiny, soft pecks. I smiled and closed my eyes as he moved down my jawline, to the space right under my ear lobes and down the right side of my neck. Pleasant prickles soared through my body as he sensuously explored my skin. He kissed the hollow of my clavicle and then moved my tank top strap down and found the front of my shoulder with his lips. I brought his face back up to mine with a gentle lift underneath his jaw and enjoyed the intimacy of our slow, deliberate kisses. It was tantalizing, and my mind wandered to a scene where I would give myself entirely to him, but I had been raised a certain way and knew I couldn't take it that far. It took everything I had inside me, but I pulled myself away from him with a breathy moan.

"Stop," I whined.

"Is everything ok?" Nolan asked between heavy breaths.

"Everything is more than okay." I stroked his hair with my wet hand. "I'm just not ready to go there with you yet."

I searched his eyes for answers. Was it okay?

"I understand completely. I'm sorry."

"No, it's not your fault."

"No, I'm sorry for letting my emotions get the better of me." He swam, leading me over to a boulder at the base of one wall, and set me down there. We were both still out of breath. Then he swam over and took a seat on a boulder near the other wall.

"You really are the most wonderful woman. The best thing that's happened to me in many years."

I melted. I thought guys usually got mad when their girlfriends denied them. But I felt the same way toward him. The exact same way.

"Ditto."

We stared at each other for a few seconds, trying to slow our breathing. His eyes always said so much to me, and right now they were forgiving eyes. "We better get out of here and dry off on the beach," I suggested.

"You're right," he said with a flirtatious smile.

We swam back around the wall and walked up onto the sand. Our blanket and things were still on the beach, seemingly untouched. Nolan bent down to inspect the bag he brought but was taking an awfully long time looking at the bottom.

"Is everything in there?" I asked, a bit concerned. I craned my neck around. We were still alone.

He took a second and then stopped looking in the bag. "Yes, everything looks okay to me." Then he closed up the bag and said, "Sorry, hon, but I hadn't expected us to go swimming, so I didn't bring any towels."

"Of course. No problem."

We laid out on the sand, allowing the rays of the sun to warm us from head to toe. Nolan held my hand as we stared off into the brilliant, cloudless sky.

I wondered what I had done to deserve the attention of such a wonderful man as Nolan Hill.

Chapter Twelve

The next week was the Fourth of July. All guides knew that before we could party that night, we had to work through a day that was certain to be hell. First of all, the day was crazy busy, which was both good and bad. Yes, more people meant more guidebooks sold, but more people also brought more trips with less breaks. You really worked your butt off on the Fourth of July. And the quality of tourists took a steep nose dive from the normal crowd.

I never figured out why, but probably more than three-fourths of the tourists on our boats on Independence Day were non-English-speaking tourists who would disregard simple onboard regulations like, "Stay seated while the boat is in motion," or "Use the garbage can on the back of the boat."

Many of these foreign passengers also believed that since they were speaking a different language, English speakers must not be able to hear them, so they speak their exotic tongue as loudly as they darn well please and whenever they want—even while their talented tour guide was talking. Fourth of July tourists were rude, loud, and messy. I know this is stereotyping, but this was my fifth summer working for the boats on the Fourth, and all my research was pointing in the same direction.

By my last tour, I was beat and had very little pep left in me. And it was on this final trip that a family with small children decided to simply move seats when their youngest puked all over the floor, leaving the mess for me to clean up when the passengers had exited the boat.

When my shift was finally over, my hair looked like a bird's nest, my shirt had sweat stains in the pits, and I felt like doing nothing but sleeping. Jack and I slowly took the steps up to street level and walked together to the parking lot. Nolan was waiting by my car. I told Jack I'd see him at the party, and then we parted ways. When I got closer to my car, I noticed Nolan was laughing at me.

"Don't ask," was all I could say. He stopped laughing and pulled me in for a hug before I could say, "Stop! I stink!"

"Wait. Let me just see here." Nolan took a whiff of my hair and said, "Yup. Just as I thought. You smell like coconuts, and it's wonderful."

I didn't think I had enough energy to smile, but somehow one showed up on my face. I gave him a quick peck on the lips. "You can always make me feel better. That's a sweet skill, you know." I pulled away from the hug and looked him in the eyes.

"So, not a great day?" He rubbed the side of my arms with his palms.

"I'll tell you all about it later tonight." I walked over to the driver's side and opened my car door. I tossed my workbag onto the front passenger seat. "I need a cold shower, and then I might just be ready to party with you tonight."

"Sounds perfect. Come over to the cabin when you're ready." He gave me a kiss and then adorably poked my nose with his finger. I climbed into my car and drove home.

There was one more thing that sucked about the Fourth of July in the Dells—the traffic! My normal, five-minute commute turned into fifteen minutes as I sat at a standstill over the Kilbourn Bridge.

When I got home, I stayed to chat with my parents for a few minutes. My dad was still doing genealogy research on the couch, so I sat down next to him.

"Hey, Dad. Have you learned anything else cool about the Gardner family?"

He shut the book and looked a little concerned. "Well, only that we've had plenty of family members die early on and many ended up in insane asylums. Sorry, kid, I think we've got bad genes." Then he laughed rather awkwardly at his own comment.

"Ah, Dad, that's pretty disturbing, actually." I wanted him to explain himself a little more. The thought of having "bad genes" inside me was making me a little uneasy.

"I'm not sure how to explain it, but from about 1913 to about 1960, several of our relatives died before the age of thirty, and many others suffered from mental disorders. But after my father died in '67, I see a bill of clean health for the Gardners. I think the 'bad genes' must have worked themselves out." He was making some notes on a legal pad on his lap.

"Huh... I hope that's true, Dad." Then I noticed a note on his paper and decided to ask him a question I never had the guts to ask before. "What about your real father? What happened to him?"

He inhaled slowly as if the pain was still with him. "I suppose you are old enough to know the truth." He shifted uncomfortably on the couch. "I was born only a few days after my father died from a unique illness. I was raised by the man you know as Grandpa Gib, who married my mother a year after my father's passing.

"As I got older, I found out Gib was not my biological father, and was naturally curious to learn more about my real dad. My mother never wanted to talk too much about it, but she did once tell me that Dad had a strange disease, and she had been trying to research a cure before he died. From that one conversation, I could tell how much she had loved my father and how she'd do anything for him." He stopped for a moment, and I could tell he was getting a little choked up.

"Gosh, I'm so sorry, Dad." I placed a hand on his forearm.

He put his hand on top of mine and then went on. "Mom was working nights sterilizing tools at a local medicine lab before my father died, hoping to come across a treatment for my father's illness. She was able to foster a great relationship with all the scientists and doctors in the county who frequented the lab. One of those men was Dr. Gib. I'm happy my mother found Gib. He was a great father to me and husband to my mother."

I leaned over and gave him a kiss on the head. "Thanks for sharing that with me, Dad. Grandma and Grandpa Gib were both amazing."

I found my mother at her sewing machine in the spare bedroom. She had spent the day making a quilt for a couple whose wedding she was attending the next weekend. I told her about my horrible day and my plans to take the party boat tonight. Mom told me Laura had come home early and was sleeping in her bedroom. Apparently she'd got a terrible headache at work and couldn't even see straight, let alone give a tour.

"Oh no! Is she still going to come to the party tonight?"

"She seemed like she still wanted to. I'm sure after her nap she'll be feeling better."

Should I tell Mom that I had been experiencing some weird headaches too? I decided against it for now. I realized I better get going, so I showered quickly and changed into jeans and a comfy black tank top. I grabbed a black hoodie as I scooted out the door.

The walk around the block seemed unusually long tonight. Perhaps I was just excited to be in Nolan's arms again.

When I arrived at his cabin door, I knocked but there was no answer. His car was parked in front, so I pushed the door open and yelled, "Hello?" as I entered. I heard the water running in the bathroom and Nolan was singing a tune I was unfamiliar with. While he was in the shower, I sat down on the loveseat by the window. His clothes were laid out on the bed and the TV was turned on to a country music channel.

Something caught my eye under the bed. It looked out of place, so I was intrigued. Curiosity possessed me, and I bent down on my hands and knees and slowly pulled a black briefcase out from under the bed. I ran my hand over the smooth top. There etched in the middle were the letters CBB. CBB? Were those initials? It had a black button lock on the front, and I traced the mechanism with my fingers.

My heart raced as I pushed in the button. The lock popped opened with what seemed like an extremely loud snap. I sat frozen and scared as I listened to hear if Nolan had heard the click from the shower. The water was still running, and he was still singing—he hadn't. I let out my breath as I slowly eased the top of the briefcase open. My jaw dropped at the sight inside.

In front of me was probably about twenty different and expensive looking mechanical gadgets: a tablet, some cell phones, an MP3 player, and something that looked like a very fancy GPS device. There were many tiny machines that I had no idea what they were for. What was this? Why would he need this gear? Was he stealing? I picked up one of the items and slowly turned it over in my hand.

Suddenly, the water from the shower shut off. My heart beat wildly. Clearly this was not meant for me to see. I dropped the little machine back in the briefcase and then carefully and very quickly shut it and slid it back under the bed. I resumed my place on the loveseat, all in a matter of a few seconds.

I couldn't breathe. My lungs felt heavy and my heart felt like it had stopped.

"Ava? Are you here?" Nolan's face peeked around the open bathroom door. I could tell he was naked, but he hid most of his muscular body behind the wall. "Hey, sweetie. I'll be out in a sec. God, you look beautiful."

The sound of his voice brought such wonderful feelings to my heart, but I was so confused. Was Nolan really whom I thought he was? I kind of wanted to get up off the couch and bolt out of there as fast as I could, but the logical side of my brain interrupted, telling me that perhaps there was a very reasonable explanation for the briefcase, and if I gave Nolan a chance to explain, he probably could.

Nolan emerged from the bathroom wearing a pair of boxer briefs. He took one look at me and knew something was wrong. "Hey, are you feeling alright? We don't have to go to the party if you don't want to. I'm more than happy to just hold up here with you." When I didn't answer he tried again. "We could throw in a movie and cuddle up on the bed." He pointed to the DVD player near the wall while he quickly jumped into a pair of shorts.

Staying in here with him was the last thing I wanted. I needed to get out into some fresh air, be around some other people, and maybe even talk this over with Laura.

When we arrived at the docks there were a ton of employees waiting around drinking beer and sitting on coolers. They were inevitably chatting about their crappy days on the river, and waiting for the time we could depart. The sun had almost set, and we knew the fireworks would be shot off soon. We all chipped in a buck for the designated driver and hopped on board the *Belle Boyd.* A few minutes later, someone untied the bow and stern lines and we were off. I spotted Laura near the front of the top deck and left Nolan with Suzanne and Brian near the back of the boat. I needed a little alone time with my little sister.

"Hey, Laura!" I said giving her a hug. "Are you feeling better? Mom told me you got a bad headache."

"Yeah. I just needed a little nap to sleep that sucker off. So did I tell you Phil let me dock the other day, and it wasn't a complete mess? Darren says I might be able to drive a few tours before summer's done!" She took a sip of her Diet Coke. "How about you, sis? How's that hot piece of arm candy working out for you?"

"Actually, I've been meaning to talk to you about him."

She smiled, grabbed my far shoulder and pulled me in for a side-hug. "You don't even have to say it, sis. It's written all over your face."

Uh-oh. It was? I was trying so hard to hide my new discovery.

"You are totally smitten by this guy! I don't think I've ever seen you like this before! I'm so happy for you!" She released me from the hug.

"Oh, right. Yes, I really do like him a lot."

Should I mention what I found under his bed? Was it the right time?

I glanced behind me and saw Nolan looking back with a smile. Oh, that look could melt me. I decided right then and there that perhaps this was the happiest I've been in my young adult life. I needed more information before I made a premature decision that would ruin my otherwise wonderful relationship with Nolan. I gave my sister another hug, thanked her (for what?), and then headed back over to Nolan.

Shortly after we took off, they drove the Belle Boyd to a spot right under the railroad bridge. It was the perfect place to watch the fireworks. I glanced to my right and saw Jack and his new girlfriend looking lovingly into each other's eyes while holding hands. Jack had been hurt in love, and at one point had given up on ever finding it again, but he took a risk, opened his heart and now was happier than I had ever seen him. What would happen if I let my guard down, too? Could I really find love again? What would happen if I dropped this wall and let Nolan into my heart, no matter who or what he was?

I didn't know what was going to happen with Nolan and me, but I did know that I wasn't ready to let go of it all.

I stood at the rail of the boat looking up into the sky while Nolan stood behind me. He wrapped his arms around my shoulders and crossed them in front of me. I grabbed his hands and held on tight as they rested across my upper chest. He pulled me in so my head and back rested on his body.

No matter how confused and scared I felt only an hour earlier, I couldn't deny the feeling I had while wrapped up carefully in Nolan's arms. Maybe we all had a few skeletons in our closets. I'm sure to come with a little baggage too. If I was truly honest with myself, I don't think I told Nolan everything about my last relationship and how scared I was to love someone again. He was willing to take whatever I wanted to give him in this relationship, and I should be happy to take what he had to offer me. So with that, I very happily spent the rest of the night by my man's side.

Chapter Thirteen

Nolan and I continued to date through the next several weeks. I was able to basically put the discovery of the briefcase out of my mind, although I noticed that the black box stayed right underneath his bed, and it seemed to be staring at me every time I was at the cabin. We spent almost every evening together and many nights, we hung out in his cabin watching old movies and playing board games. It was so simple, yet so perfect.

The other evenings were spent doing very traditional Dells tourist activities. I took him to the famous Tommy Bartlett Ski Sky and Stage extravaganza, we saw the magic show, danced in the street to a live band playing downtown, tried out many of the mini-golf courses, hit the movie theater, tasted fare at the farmer's market, and even got an Old Time Photo taken. I was wearing a flapper outfit and he wore a gangster suit. He held a bottle of whisky, and I got to hold a fake gun. It was all so much fun! I felt so comfortable with myself around him, and we seemed to complement each other so well.

As August came into view, Nolan had given me no other reason not to trust him, so I quit worrying about the briefcase, and I concentrated on enjoying the time I had to spend with Nolan.

I realized I had been so focused on Nolan that I hadn't checked in with Kasie in a while. I called several times on different days and it always went to voicemail. I sent a text, which went unanswered for a few days until I finally got a reply:

Sorry girl! No time to talk! Had to take another shift at the pool and got a night job waitressing downtown. Maybe I'll be able to pay for next semester now.

I was pretty sure that was her way of asking if my grades were okay, but I didn't give her the bad news. *Good for you! But don't work yourself into the ground,* I replied.

There was so much I hadn't talked to Kasie about. Come to think of it, most of the summer flew by and I didn't mention that Nolan and I were even dating. I decided to hold off that information until I was able to tell her in person; plus summer was more than half over, and although I didn't like it, I was pretty sure my time with Nolan was limited. Even though it was constantly on my mind, that was one thing we never really talked about—what was going to happen when I had to go back to school? Would Nolan be ready for a long-distance relationship? Because I certainly didn't want to end things soon. Would he be willing to relocate to Stevens Point? There seemed to be nothing keeping him here in this area of Wisconsin.

Part of me wanted so desperately to bring the subject up, but at the same time, I couldn't find the guts within me to do it. What if he wanted to end the whole relationship right then and there? I didn't know if I could handle hearing those words. I wanted to squeeze out as many days of bliss as I could before I inevitably had to face the music at the end of the month. But part of me was wondering—wasn't he thinking the same thing? Maybe he felt like I did and just didn't know the answer.

One night we fell asleep cuddling together on his bed in the cabin, and when I woke up, it was two in the morning. I thought the end of my life was near as I sprinted through the yards separating Animal Island from my parents' house. My mother had thankfully fallen asleep waiting for me in the Lazy Boy in the living room. I was able to sneak in the front door, quietly ascend the stairs, change into pajamas, and climb into bed without her waking up. The next morning, I smoothed everything over by telling her we'd had a conversation at 12:30 when I got home, but she must have been out of it since she couldn't remember.

Things at work were certainly picking up. Jack and I were selling a lot of tour books and making some good money. Jack's tricks were getting more complicated—fake poop on the floor, balloons flying out of the back closet, the good ol' whoopee cushion trick, and many others. One time he even tried the paper on the window trick again. Although this time he had written, "There's a bomb on the boat!" and before I could even read the paper, it flew off the window and tumbled into the crowd.

"Oh crap!" I heard Jack say from downstairs. Then his head appeared in the hatch. "Get that paper! NOW!"

I turned around to find it had stuck to a middle-aged lady's face and she pulled the paper off with disgust. I giggled a little under my breath and then apologized and asked for the paper. Before she could hand it over to me, her husband read the message, and he stood up yelling,

"There's a bomb on the boat!" Panic ensued as many passengers tried to file down the aisle.

I just about screamed over the microphone: "Stop! Stop! Please return to your seat!" Then I calmed my voice down a bit and said, "Ladies and gentlemen, I assure you we are in no danger! Please sit down, and I will explain!" Many of the passengers settled down and returned to their seats, but a few had escaped down the back stairs and were contemplating jumping out the gate on the back deck. "Ladies and gentlemen. Please, return to your seats immediately. You see, Captain Jack is a bit of a jokester and tries to make me laugh every day. This is one of his pranks, obviously gone wrong. I assure you we are in no danger."

I sang an extra song for the crowd that tour and put on the most charming personality I could muster up. I wasn't trying to sell extra books, but simply making sure they were happy and not ready to report this to Darren. We got gotched again, but this time we knew it was of our own doing. We actually had a good laugh about it after the tour.

Jack was in the best of moods as his new relationship seemed to be going about as smoothly as mine was. One day he invited her on one of our trips. Natalie joined him in the quest to make me laugh during our tour. I was up on the top deck of the boat, and when I came down, she was sitting in the front row wearing a bright orange life jacket and pretending to brush her teeth with a wire brush we used for cleaning. It rated mild on the joke scale, but I was thrilled that she was joining in on the fun. Natalie was great, and I was so happy for Jack. It was really starting to feel like love was in the air down at the Lower Dells this summer.

But as August came to a close, our future was sitting in the back of my mind. I contemplated not returning to college, but I knew my parents would be disappointed, and I knew I should probably give it another year. It was less than a week before I had to go off to school again, and Nolan had no plans to report of. I wondered why he couldn't simply make a decision about what he wanted to do with his life. It was frustrating me beyond belief. He was twenty years old, for goodness sake. A few times I researched jobs and college programs in the Stevens Point area and tried to share the websites with him. He was very good at changing the subject and never really looking into any of my suggestions.

One day during the last week before school started again, I went up to Lower Two after my first tour to say hi to Nolan. I knew the second I entered the door that something was horribly wrong. His posture was off and he looked incredibly nervous.

My lungs felt like they had collapsed in my chest. "Hey, honey, are you okay?" I went over to him and put my hands around his waist. He kissed my forehead and then pulled away. It was a courtesy kiss.

He looked deep into my eyes as if he was trying to see right into my brain. "I'm good now. When are you off tonight?" But his voice was all wrong; something wobbled behind his voice box. Why were his eyes red and glossed over?

"We're the first boat today. Our last trip's at 5:15." I grabbed his hand. Something was definitely not right.

He moved in for a hug and whispered in my ear. I could barely hear him. "We can't talk here but you need to trust me when I say this..." But a middle-aged couple with some loud kids walked up to the booth at that moment and he quickly pulled away from me.

What? What was he saying? Nothing was making sense.

When the family left he said, "Can you come over when you are done with work? I've got...ah, something planned." He smiled but it wasn't the genuine smile I was used to. He was definitely covering, afraid to say what he needed to say.

He pulled me in again. "I can't wait for this day to go by." Then he kissed my forehead once more before some more customers approached the window. I had an uneasy feeling in my stomach.

The day ticked by so slowly, and it seemed that every time I went up to talk with Nolan, he looked more and more sick. He was continuously swamped with customers all day and we didn't get to talk at all. I just needed a sign that everything was okay but I got nothing from him except a strange foreshadowing that heartache was right around the corner.

My heart felt like it was in overdrive all day, and by the time my last tour had finished, I was exhausted. I swept the boat in record speed, paid Jack for his share of the books sales, and then sprinted down the dock and up the stairs to street level. When I glanced back at Lower Two, I saw that it was closed up. I waved bye to Brian as I ran past Lower One and down the sidewalk to the parking lot.

I didn't even stop at home to change. I drove directly to Animal Island and parked next to Nolan's cabin. His car wasn't there. I went up to the door and knocked and yelled for him, but there was no answer. The cabin was locked, and when I pressed my ear to the door, I didn't hear a sound. I didn't know what to do, so I walked around the back of the cabin, and that's when I noticed the window right next to his bed was broken. I examined it and saw blood and tiny pieces of flesh stuck to the shards of glass.

I stood there stunned, confused, and panicked. Who was this man and what was going on? My body didn't know what to do except drop to my knees and cry. I put my head in my hands and let the tears flow through my fingers and onto the unmown grass.

The briefcase! I should have confronted him!

It was almost fifteen minutes before Nolan found me. "Ava? What's wrong? Are you alright?" He knelt down on the grass beside me and put his arms around my back. I wanted to throw them off me, but instead I let his arms pull me into his chest, and I melted into his body. He smelled so wonderfully, and his touch made me feel so safe. A million emotions flooded my heart. I was so scared, yet so in love with this man. I sat up and tried to look at him through watery eyes.

"Please, sweet Ava, tell me, are you hurt?" He brushed a flyaway piece of hair from my nose and held my face in his hands. I looked up at his eyes and saw they were filled with tears as well, and his left eye was all bruised and bloodshot. He kissed me hard and sweet. I gave into him, kissing him back with all my emotions, tears still streaming down my cheeks. Then, suddenly, he picked me up in his arms and carried me to the front of his cabin. He placed me in the front seat of his car, got in, and peeled away from Animal Island, spraying gravel everywhere.

He didn't say a word as he sped down Minnesota Avenue past the post office and around the back of the swimming pool. I quietly sobbed as the summer sun was setting beneath the trees. He parked next to the baseball fields. Make Out Rock. He was taking me to the site of our first kiss. He shut off the ignition but stayed in the car, staring out the windshield with anger and frustration splashed across his face.

"I don't want this to end. This *has* to end." It was like two people were fighting in his head.

I didn't know what he meant. Was he breaking up with me?

"I don't want this to end either." I reached for his hand, but he jerked it away. None of it added up. If he could just tell me what was going on...

He dropped his head into his hands and mumbled something I couldn't make out. Then he lifted his head and screamed to the ceiling of the car, "I just can't do it!"

"What?" I screamed back. This was it. This was the end. My heart cracked into a thousand pieces. What had I done to bruise this relationship?

Then he completely changed demeanor, like he had found the answer in his head. He leaned over and whispered to me, "Say nothing. Let's get out of here." He opened the car door, and I followed his instructions. He impatiently waited for me to come around the front of the car, and then he grabbed my hand and held on tightly. He pulled me until we were running towards Make Out Rock.

A train's loud horn rang out down the tracks several hundred yards away. "Perfect," he said. We jumped over the train tracks and ran the deep path until we were at the rock cliff. I turned to see the train speed by right as he grabbed me firmly by the shoulders and turned to look me straight in the eye.

His face was within inches of mine. "I don't have much time." The train was so loud he was yelling.

"What is going on? Tell me right now!" I screamed between sobs. "Nolan, I love you. You can tell me anything!" I willed his eyes to speak to me; they were flooded with tears again. The train wailed behind us.

"I love you, too." Then he kissed me filled with emotion, but there was obvious confliction behind it. I held onto his lower back tightly, not wanting to ever let go. We could just stay on the rock forever, happily kissing, and everything would be okay.

Then it happened. He pulled away, looked me straight in the eyes, and with a shaken voice he said, "I'm so sorry it has to be this way. I truly do love you, Ava Gardner," and then he let out a grunt, and I heard a strange metallic clinking sound as something fell to the stony ground. I yelled his name, but then doubled over in hysterics as I saw Nolan running away from me without looking back. As if he had timed it perfectly, he crossed the train tracks just as the caboose sped by and he ran off into the darkness.

My head began to pound violently. Why did this heartache feel like I was dying? I tried to tell myself to stand, to get my body up and pathetically return home defeated and broken.

The tears came down like a rainstorm as pain radiated through my whole body. I was convulsing and shaking, and abruptly felt extremely cold. Then came an excruciating pain in my side. I slid a hand down to my torso and, to my surprise, I felt a wet and sticky liquid.

Something shiny caught the moon's ray on the rock a few feet away. It was a knife about three inches long. My bright red blood was slowly sliding down the flat layers of rock to the place where the knife was.

Nolan had stabbed me.

He was gone.

I knew in that instant that I did not want to live this messed-up life anymore. I was ready for death. So I let myself slip into the darkness in front of me.

Part Two

Chapter One

It was late afternoon when I arrived at the cabin I'd be staying in while working in the Dells. I parked my silver Audi in a short gravel driveway and stared at the site before me—a few broken-down, olive green, and incredibly small cabins sitting in a bed of overgrown grass.

I let out a loud sigh as I pulled my key from the ignition, but stayed in the car a moment, thinking. I looked around. So this would be my home for a while. I guessed it wouldn't be so bad.

I thought back to the unexpected events of my day—especially the Lower Dells boat tour when I first caught sight of Ava. She had displayed the kind of striking beauty that seemed to come naturally, like she didn't have to work hard at it. I smiled at the thought of her.

You have a job to do this summer, Nolan. Getting a girl is not an option, my brain scolded. I shook my head trying to get the picture of Ava from my mind.

I grabbed my cell and the ring of keys Darren had given me from the console, and then got out of the car. Behind me there was a row of five more cabins identical to mine, but there wasn't a soul in sight. It was eerily quiet.

I popped the trunk and took out my black work briefcase and the luggage I had packed that morning in Chicago before I left. It was unclear how long I'd be on this mission, so I had to pack as if I'd be here for three months.

Ava popped into my mind again. Her body was fit and she had nicely toned legs. All of that was wonderful, but her smile was the most gorgeous thing I had ever seen. My mind's eye could clearly see her soft brown eyes under her long dark eyelashes. They were sweet, caring eyes that matched perfectly with her thin pink lips.

I slammed the trunk shut.

So what? She's gorgeous. I can look, right? Just as long as I keep my heart out of it.

A worn path through the grass led to two wooden steps leading up to cabin three. I pulled open the holey screen door and swatted at a moth as it fluttered past my face, freed from the door's captivity. The key fit awkwardly in the hole and I had to use some muscle to get it to turn, but eventually I got the old wooden door open with a creak.

The light on the ceiling flickered when I flipped the switch, and as I took a step into the small space my nose instantly filled with a musty smell. When was the last time anyone stayed in this cabin? The air felt stale and the whole thing was in need of a deep cleaning.

Hopefully I wouldn't be here too long.

I set my bags down on the floor and sat on the couch across from the twin bed. Six bright blue Dells Boat Tour bumper stickers had been haphazardly slapped onto the wall outside the bathroom. My mind flipped back to my first boat tour. I had sat on the bottom deck waiting for the tour to begin, and had had the perfect vantage point to watch Ava untie the front of the boat. She leaned far over the rail on the dock and I followed her long, muscular, tanned legs all the way up the back of her shorts.

Damn.

Ava threw the rope onto the bow and I craned my neck, watching her walk all the way to the back of the dock.

"She's single, if you were wondering."

I snapped my head back towards Jack.

Woops. Busted.

I smiled and Jack flashed a mischievous grin back at me.

It would be hard to ignore this woman. I had absolutely no intentions coming into it, but my heart argued that perhaps this summer didn't have to be all business. My brain intervened: *Don't even think about it, Nolan. This is work. You could be leaving at anytime.*

My phone buzzed in my hand, jolting me back to the present. *New text message from Agent Harper.* I slid my finger across the screen to receive the message.

Intelligence indicates the source of radiation is within a 200-mile radius of your area. Continue ruse and stand by for further instructions.

A nervous bubble swelled in my stomach, but I quickly pushed it away. This was my first mission as a field agent, and I was not about to mess it up. A lot was riding on me being successful here, and I knew that for now my job was to lie low and play the ticket agent part for a while.

The Boat Tours had supplied some furnishings within the cabin including a limited supply of used cooking utensils and dishes in the kitchen, an overly soft couch, a hard twin bed, and, thankfully, a small flat-screen TV mounted to the wall outside the bathroom. I turned on the tube and it was set to a channel broadcasting commercials for attractions in the Dells. Before I could turn the channel, a big blue and white tour boat glided over the river through some tall, rocky cliffs.

"The Rocky Island Region," I remembered from Ava's tour. I was taken back to our conversation on the bottom deck of the General Bailey on the way back upstream, when I had been rendered speechless by Ava's very presence.

I was losing my nerve. I couldn't look her in the eye. I tried to remember my stress training. Could any of that apply here?

"Keep talking," my heart instructed.

I managed to mutter something about cornfields.

Idiot! What are you, some kind of hick? Come on, pull it together and say something intelligent!

"Are you from the area? It's so beautiful here."

Well, that wasn't half bad. Showing some interest is good.

I glanced quickly at her face. She was still talking, but I couldn't hear a word she was saying over the loud beating of my heart.

God, she was beautiful.

I swallowed hard, suddenly aware of my increasingly sweaty armpits and wondered if my cologne was too strong. I felt a bead of sweat falling from my hairline, so I nonchalantly looked out the window to wipe the sweat away and get myself under control.

I had been trained to stay as cool as ice in high-pressure situations, but somehow, Ava had some kind of power over me that was taking precedence. If some young college girl from small-town Wisconsin could affect me like this, what would I do when I was faced with real danger?

Dread filled my heart. I was failing at the very job I hadn't even begun yet.

I continued to hide by looking out the window, thinking back to the last nine months in Chicago surrounded by underground offices, tall, urban buildings, and lots and lots of grey. The natural world around me was so refreshing. Part of my job would be to protect it.

Was I really ready for the career path I had chosen for myself? I knew it would be a life of loneliness, but the deeply rooted loyalty I felt for this country consumed my heart so overwhelmingly. My parents had had a large part in leading me down this career path. They had always been extremely patriotic and selfless in everything they did.

Being here now was only part of a minor mission—a way for the agency to see if I was worthy for the big leagues. All my hard work proving myself had brought me here.

During the boat tour I had noticed a classic all-American family sitting on the shoreline fishing—mom, dad, two kids, and a dog. They had a picnic spread out on a red and white checkered cloth and were laughing and splashing in the river water, completely unaware of the thousands of people behind the scenes that had committed themselves to defending and protecting the American public from real and horrific threats everyday.

This was what I was meant to do.

So I got to work. I entered my security code on the lock on my briefcase and it popped open with a loud click. My tablet was near the top of the collection of items inside, and it didn't take me long to set up a hotspot and connect to the Internet. I pulled up my op files and began to review my mission.

Task Mission #23322: Assist in locating and identifying hazardous environmental threats to the health and safety of the American people by searching area environments and interacting with locals, extrapolating any relevant information and reporting it to the proper authorities of the CBB offices.

Pretty broad. I read on.

The agency has deployed agents in areas throughout the Midwest posing as false employees for various cooperatives around Wisconsin, Illinois, Minnesota, and Michigan. All agents are to be ready to act as soon as intelligence acquires enough information to support the intended mission.

It would likely be many weeks, maybe months, for the agency to narrow down the area further, but nevertheless, we were to stay alert, keen to our task, and in shape.

An hour later I changed into some mesh shorts and a T-shirt for a run. I wanted to be in top physical shape in preparation for any kind of physical demand I may encounter. I had to prove myself to the agency. This was one job I wasn't going to mess up.

Chapter Two

I am an agent for the FBI.

I've always been somewhat of a brainiac. My parents and teachers decided I should skip the third grade. When I was seventeen I went to Northwestern University in Chicago and got an undergraduate degree in International Law in only three years. I'd always thought law was interesting, but didn't think I would ever become a lawyer; it was just something to study for the time being.

While in college I became fluent in three languages, and at twenty I graduated summa cum laude. School had always come easy to me, and although I was younger than most of my peers, my personality and charm enabled me to thrive in any learning environment. I'm one of those geeks that everyone loves to hate because I didn't really ever need to study, but I always got A's. It's like my brain takes a picture of the textbook or lecture, and I can remember it clear as day later on. Although I did take school seriously, I had my fun in college too, keeping a few good buddies and dating casually, but nothing stuck.

I still wasn't sure what I wanted to do with my life, so I went back to Northwestern to study for a master's degree in genetics, another subject I found interesting. Two years later I was studying my notes at a wooden picnic table in the park when, out of the blue, I was recruited by FBI Agent Harper and offered a job in a special sector deep within the agency. I was shocked. Although my parents had always modeled the value of national pride, I had never considered a career in national security.

It meant major sacrifices in my life, including assuming a fake life to fool the people closest to me. I really did love my family and friends, and I would feel horrible having to keep such a secret from them. I was given one week to make a decision, and I don't think I slept a wink those seven days. In the end, I figured I had nothing to lose. I had no real plans for my life at that moment, and I felt an overwhelming feeling that the FBI was my calling.

Even though I do like my job, my life has been relatively secret to those I am closest to. I often find I am living two lives, which isn't always the most convenient. To be honest, it can be very lonely.

I've been in training and working in Chicago for the last two years. Very early on, I was chosen to be a part of a special Clandestine Biomonitoring Branch of the Bureau. This section employs environmental biologists, genetic scientists, and neurologists trained to examine the lives Americans live and look for vulnerabilities in our environment that may cause health risks or other threats to the American people.

I find this type of work very interesting, but I had worked in the office for the majority of my time with the CBB thus far. For the past half a year I had been allowed to begin my survival, torture, and combat training. It was strenuous and exhausting, but at the same time thrilling. I was excited to start work as a field agent.

Less than a month ago, the CBB intercepted some information indicating there may be a non-urgent public health risk in the Midwest. I have not been made privy to the complete details, but I know the concern is related to low levels of possibly harmful radiation being passed through the environment by one source.

Through their research, the CBB had narrowed the source of emissions down to several areas and sent an agent undercover to each of these areas for the summer. The experts were working back at headquarters in Chicago and at other stations around the country continuing their research. As information became evident, we were supposed to be updated.

So here I was at my undercover job as Dells Boat Tours ticket agent. On one hand I longed to be back at headquarters shooting guns and practicing my combat skills, and on the other hand I was on an actual mission. My first mission.

Darren had me shadowing various ticket agents in booths around town. Most days I was bored out of my mind, training for a job I expected to be at only temporarily. Some days it was hard to pay attention. I spent a lot of that time on my phone texting other guys at the agency, trying to get some info on what they were up to. A few guys were still in Chicago, training and waiting for their tasks to be assigned. Some were luckier, posted to other parts of the country, kicking ass behind the scenes.

One day I was assigned to train with this cool guy, Brian. Brian was a nineteen-year-old with broad shoulders and a thin waist. He had dark hair and eyes, and a very friendly face. Brian and I shared the same sense of humor, poking fun at tourists behind their backs and being goofy. Working and learning from Brian was so refreshing. It had been so long since I'd felt so free.

I could tell Brian was genuinely a good guy. We talked a lot about sports that day in the ticket booth right next to the downtown Dairy Queen. I even learned some good tips on how to be a profitable ticket agent. I didn't really care about making money, of course, but he was so good, I couldn't help picking up a few tricks. Brian was the first agent to trust me enough to let me sell tickets on his shift while he sat back with his feet up on the ticket counter.

Brian told me this was his fourth year working for the boats, and so they placed him mostly at the best booth, Lower One. He probably knew a lot about Ava, and I wanted so badly to ask him about her, but something made me stop. I knew in the back of my mind that the agency would frown upon field agents engaging in personal activity during their mission—but my mission hadn't really been defined yet. I was basically staking out our territory while the guys in the lab on the other side of the country did the real research. They weren't even sure of the exact location or the actual severity of the threat yet.

But oh, those big brown eyes...

A police car sped down Broadway with its lights and sirens on, breaking up my daydream. People stopped on the sidewalks to watch it speed by for a second, and then they went back to their business of vacationing. The sidewalks on both sides of the street were filled with people of all ages shopping, eating, and buying tickets from Brian.

I decided I could use a friend in this crazy tourist town, especially if I was going to be here all summer. "Hey, Brian, whadaya say I pick up some beer on the way home, and we head over to the Island to relax a bit?"

He looked at me like I was crazy. Did I say something wrong?

"Ah buddy...? How old are you? You look like you're about nineteen."

Oh shoot.

I forgot I'm supposed to be almost twenty. One reason the agency picked me for this assignment was because, although I was twenty-four, my facial features made me look twenty as long as I kept clean-shaven.

"Naw, I'll be twenty at the end of the summer. Hey, I bet you're not into drinking. You play football at UW–Whitewater, right?"

"Yeah. Gotta keep this machine in perfect working order, so I stay away from alcohol." He flexed his biceps. "You wanna join me for a workout tomorrow morning?"

I probably should keep up on my weight training while I was waiting for the action. "Yeah, give me a call in the morning before you leave."

After work, I had to visit the Boat office to restock my ticket briefcase. As I drove down the hill by the Lower Dells, Ava's pretty face flashed before my mind. I stopped at the stoplight, wondering how my brief encounter with her a few days before could have left such a lasting impression. The light turned green and I took a left, past the docks. Curiously, I studied the parking lot, wondering if I could catch a glimpse of Ava leaving work.

There she was, sitting on a park bench, staring out over the river.

Acting on an impulse, I switched on my left blinker and waited for oncoming traffic to clear. I watched her sitting there, imagining sitting next to her with my arm around her shoulders.

What the hell am I thinking? I'm here for work this summer, not for romance.

I switched my blinker off and glanced over my right shoulder to merge back into traffic, but a sudden rush of cars forced me to wait, and provided me time to look back at Ava.

Where'd she go?

I searched the parking lot, but didn't see her anywhere. Then my heart shifted into high gear when I spotted her hop the safety fence.

What the hell was she doing? Was she going to jump down the hill? It's probably sixty feet down!

"No! Ava!" I yelled. I had to stop her!

I rampantly took advantage of a tiny space between oncoming traffic and sped into DBT's parking lot. I threw my Audi into park in a handicapped stall and rushed over to Ava just as she almost toppled down the hill. With no seconds to spare I caught hold of her backpack and grabbed her tiny waist, lifting her onto the wooden railing.

Holy crap! That was close.

She looked up at me, stunned, and muttered something incoherent. She was scared, her arms and legs shaking. She was so innocently gorgeous. I wanted to wrap her in my arms and make her feel safe. I grabbed her hand instead. It felt mildly appropriate.

But in the next second anger washed over me and I inadvertently scolded her. Why would she put herself in danger that way? The intense desire to pull Ava close, and the fear I felt for her safety scared me. I barely knew this woman.

You're here for work, Nolan, my brain reminded myself. *Leave now.*

"I'm glad you're okay. I've gotta head to the Boat office."

Dammit, she's so beautiful.

"Take care of yourself, Ava. I'd like to see you around here again."

Get out of here, Nolan, before you're in too deep.

Chapter Three

One morning, five days into my stint in the Dells, I received an email from my boss, Agent Harper, detailing the lack of progress in my mission, as nothing had developed, and it looked like I'd be playing the part of ticket agent for the whole summer. I was okay with that. If I had to jump through a few hoops to land a bit higher on the ladder, then that's what I was ready and willing to do.

Agent Harper's email also indicated that he'd arranged for me to take the next day off from work at DBT and was to report to the CBB offices in Chicago. I went to sleep that night excited for a twist in what had become a somewhat mundane routine in the Dells and to spend the day training and getting briefed at the CBB office.

I left at an ungodly hour early in the morning in order to make the four-hour drive into Chicago and land at the office's front step by 9 A.M. I survived on three large coffees and a bag of chocolate mini doughnuts. Oh, and my favorite talk-radio station.

A few times my mind wandered to the day before, when Ava and Jack came up to visit Lower One during their break. Before I knew it, I had somewhat scolded Ava for almost tumbling down the hill into the river, but she apologized sweetly, not bothered by my reprimand.

Being so close to her really stirred up some feelings inside me and thinking about it now scared me a little. I could not let some petty feelings for a woman I barely know get in the way of my career aspirations.

No more thoughts of Ava today, my brain threatened my heart.

"Fine," I said out loud. "She's gone. Clear head."

The parking garage was noticeably empty as I pulled into one of the first stalls. I wondered if half the agency was off for some reason. It felt good to be back at the office. Although I had only been gone about a week, there had been a sliver of homesickness present in my heart. I pulled on my suit coat before I shut the car door and took a deep breath of city air.

I swiped my ID card at the door and entered the passcodes outside the elevator. The CBB offices were located on the fifteenth through twenty-fifth floors of a Chicago-based bank building. I was told the employees of the bank thought the execs inhabited those floors and, as a rule, stayed away.

I took the elevator up to CBB's reception and checked in. "Agent Hill, reporting for Agent Harper," I told the pretty blond at the desk. Three oversized, silvery letters spelled out CBB on the wall behind her head. Upon closer look, I noticed the words *North Central* under the large letters.

"Agent Hill," she smiled brightly, "Credentials, please."

I handed over my ID card and badge. She swiped them over the scanner built into the desk and held onto them as the results popped onto the computer screen. "Agent Harper is expecting you." She leaned forward to reach something at the back of her desk and I got an eyeful of her cleavage. I looked away politely as she put a small tablet and stylus on the high counter in front of me. "Please sign here and enter your passcode."

I did as she said and returned the device. She traded it for my credentials.

"Your agenda for the day has been uploaded to your phone. Please take the A Elevators up to the locker rooms as you'll be training within the hour."

"Thank you," I replied, gathering my briefcase from the floor.

"Have a nice day, Agent Hill."

"You too, ma'am."

The A Elevators were all the way at the end of the hall. I pressed the up button and found the agenda on my phone as I waited for the elevator doors to open. In thirty minutes I was to be changed and ready in the training arena found on the sixteenth floor for rifle and assault training until noon. It looked like I'd have a break for lunch and then spend the afternoon at intelligence getting briefed on any updates with the current mission.

I smiled. It felt good to be back.

There were a few other agents in the arena when I arrived. I didn't know any of them by name, but recognized their faces. We engaged in small talk while we waited for our instructor to arrive.

"Good morning, agents," a man called as he entered the cavernous room. He took several hard steps on the concrete floor and then his gait gained a little bounce as he walked onto the mat covering most of the arena. He was a tall man with square shoulders and tight muscles on every inch of his body. His long black hair had been pulled back into a tight ponytail at the back of his head.

"Oh great," the guy next to me muttered. "Agent Miller. He's a hard ass."

I groaned quietly. I'd be sore tomorrow for sure.

Agent Miller reached the middle of the arena. "I'm Agent Miller, new to this division, but I'm sure you'll find me suitable for your needs. We'll begin with combat training. Let's get to work, boys."

* * * *

Just as predicted, training was tough and by lunch I felt exhausted. We spent an hour and a half in combat training with Agent Miller and then we were sent to the gun range where we sharpened our shooting. Afterward I took a nice long shower and then relaxed in the agents' lounge before I had to report to intelligence.

The afternoon turned out to be a complete opposite of the morning—drab, uninteresting, and very slow moving. I sat through two policy meetings and no sliver of amusement came until midway through the second meeting when we heard shouting in the hallway.

"It's all a hoax!" a man's voice yelled. "You're being fooled!"

The agent presenting to us rose quickly from his chair and jumped to the door. I caught a glimpse of a suited agent struggling to break free from the hold of two other agents trying to escort the man down the hall.

"That's enough," replied a stern voice. Two electronic darts shot from a guard's stun gun and stuck to the man's torso. He let out a series of grunts and then fell to the ground, limp, just as the door to the conference room shut.

"That was odd," I whispered to the agent next to me.

"That's Agent Hicks," he whispered back. "He's been talking crazy for weeks. They would have sacked him before now, but he's a genius, and they need him."

"Let us continue on, shall we?" the agent in charge suggested.

Finally, by late afternoon, I met with intelligence to be briefed on my mission. But that was anticlimactic because there was nothing really to report. We were still searching for a source of radiation somewhere in the Midwest.

They must know more, I thought as I drove back to the Dells that evening. The FBI has some of the most high-tech equipment in the world. Why couldn't they narrow down the source of radiation more easily?

But I wasn't about to lose sleep over it now. I was more than excited to be on my first mission, be it boring as all hell. That night my aching body slept like a baby.

Chapter Four

It wasn't long before I settled into my job as ticket agent. I spent a few days working at different booths uptown and there I got a chance to read some reports Agent Harper had required me to review. I was able to sneak my tablet under the ticket counter at a booth called Upper Ducks, and even if I left my hotspot in the cabin, I could hook up to some Wi-Fi from a nearby coffee shop. It all worked out perfectly.

But as much as I tried, I couldn't shake Ava's pretty face from my mind, so I was very happy when Darren expressed how impressed he was with my selling skills. This meant I would be scheduled at Lower One or Two most days, and, in turn, I would see Ava. I liked working with Brian and Suzanne, too. They were both a blast to be around. It was a nice change from the suit-wearing, stuck-up nerds hanging around headquarters.

Ava gradually began spending more and more time visiting the booth on her breaks. I knew I initially had a physical attraction to Ava, but the more I got to know her, the more I began to utterly adore her sweet personality and irresistible laughter. We played off each other well and had the same sense of humor.

But each time my heart opened up a little more, my brain was there with a rebuttal. *You're not here for romance.*

However, things with the agency were moving pretty slow. It might be okay if I explored a relationship with Ava.

If only for the summer.

So that's why I took the risk one afternoon when Darren sent me out to the Delton Corners ticket booth unexpectedly part way through my shift. I was really disappointed. I hadn't even gotten to talk to Ava yet, and now that I had to leave, I wouldn't be around when the *General Bailey* returned to the docks.

On a whim, I took a piece of scrap paper and wrote a note for Ava. Maybe she would come out to see me after work.

Don't do it, my brain protested as I handed Suzanne the note.

"Could you please make sure Ava gets this?" I asked her, ignoring my brain. She grabbed it with a sneaky smile on her face.

"What's it say?"

I took the money and tickets out of the drawer and packed up my briefcase. "I bet you could guess."

Suzanne threw out her hip and placed her right hand on top of it. "Oh, Nolan, don't you think she's a little out of your league?"

I swallowed hard. That was flat-out rude. I turned around to look at her. "What do you mean by that?"

Suzanne was known to say precisely what was on her mind, even if it wasn't exactly the most appropriate thing to say to someone's face. "I don't want you to get your heart broken." She placed the note on her stool and handed me my phone from the counter.

No matter how hurtful Suzanne came off, her comments couldn't be as damaging as my own insecurities. "Just give her the letter. See you tomorrow."

I left the booth and headed toward the parking lot. There was a great view of the river and power dam on the south side of the lot, and I stopped to take a look and think for a moment. It was this exact place where I rescued Ava from tumbling down the rocky hillside. Even if Ava was too good for me to date, she at least could use someone watching out for her safety. I noticed the Bailey coming in and instantly felt disappointed. I had just missed Ava. She was standing by the gate on the back deck holding the rope in her hands, waiting to tie up the boat. Soon she'd be up at the booth, possibly looking for me.

Seeing Ava made my heart beat quicker. I put Suzanne's comments out of my head for the time being and reluctantly headed off to my car.

I hopped in my Audi and drove ten minutes or so down Highway 12, all the way out to Lake Delton. I parked in the lot by the Delton Corners ticket booth and shut off the engine. I had a few hours to wait before Ava could come visit, if she even decided to come out to the booth, so I took my CBB briefcase inside, expecting to get some agency work done.

It wasn't long before I was deep into an essay on the types of harmful radiation found on earth. Although radiation naturally occurs within our bodies from birth, we also receive a small dose from space and sometimes larger doses from the earth itself. The agency was sure the background radiation they were detecting was terrestrial, or found deep within the earth. They wanted to pinpoint the source before they contracted drillers and started ripping up the Midwest. It was more than the commonplace radon gas that forms naturally from radioactive elements that decay in our soil. No, this was stronger, more deadly.

I traced my fingers over a recent map of the Midwest in my file. There were several areas colored-coded according to their levels of harmful radiation. Much of Wisconsin, Illinois, and Minnesota showed the highest levels.

I flipped to another document provided by the agency. It was a chart indicating the levels of radiation commonly released by certain radioactive materials. There were several dozen elements, all naturally occurring on the earth. I scanned the list twice, reading all the levels.

Something didn't seem right.

I turned back to the map. The levels of radiation in certain areas on the map were much higher than any of the levels in the chart of terrestrial elements. Much, much higher.

"The radiation isn't terrestrial," I said out loud. "Cosmic. It has to be cosmic."

I grabbed my tablet and researched levels of radiation from heavily charged space particles and gamma rays.

"That's closer." I flipped between the map and the chart of cosmic radiation levels. "We're not looking for something deep within the ground! We should be searching for something fallen from space, probably on the surface of the earth!"

I popped up, ready to perform my best touch-down dance when a light blue Oldsmobile pulled into the parking lot, the driver's brown hair touching epaulettes on the shoulders of her white button-down shirt.

Ava!

I scrambled to put away my documents and heard the bell ring over the door just as the last of my things were hidden. Ava was standing in the doorway. She came to see me!

Chapter Five

The minute Ava left Delton Corners I pulled out my work documents and checked the numbers again. Could I really have made an integral discovery? I dialed the agency's number with excitement fluttering through my stomach. Agent Harper would be so proud of me.

But then a stroke of insecurity fell across my heart before I hit *send*.

I put down my cell phone and picked up the map, scanning it again. Why hadn't any of the geniuses at the agency noticed this discrepancy before? Maybe they had and reporting this would make me look like an idiot.

I paced back and forth behind the ticket counter. I was trained as a field agent, ready to protect the American people from such threats as organized crime, civil rights violators, or drug trafficking. I wasn't supposed to be the one to make a discovery like this. My assignment was to passively hold my post until instructed to do otherwise.

I stopped pacing and picked up the phone. Even if the CBB already knew about the cosmic radiation, I had to make sure. I asked for Agent Harper, but reception said he couldn't be reached. I considered sending an email, but it seemed like the type of information I should deliver on a secure line. Nevertheless, this discovery could wait overnight. I'd call him when the sun rose.

With my work mind somewhat at rest, I began thinking of Ava and replaying the brochure rack scene over in my head. The more I relived it, the more adorable Ava became to me. I wondered what she was doing at her parent's house. Probably counting the huge stack of cash she earned guiding today. I pulled open my till drawer and counted how many tickets I had sold at this booth: two. I couldn't imagine why the boat company kept this booth open. It was the epitome of slow. I reread all of the newest documents the CBB had sent me, just to make sure I wasn't making some kind of mistake. Finally eight o'clock rolled around, and my shift officially ended.

When I got home there were several employees sitting around the bonfire pit, so I stopped to talk to a few of them for a while just to be nice. I hadn't spent too much time outside my cabin since I moved in, so as I sat by the fire, I took in my surroundings. Someone had nailed a sign that read "Animal Island" to the tree near the front drive. I wondered what that meant. The back of the land butted up to an alley running through the middle of the small block. We could see the backs of a few houses, and I could see straight through to the next street over—Capital Street, I think.

Something caught my eye on that street directly through the yards and trees. Parked in front of a two-story, green house was a light blue Oldsmobile Cutlass Sierra that looked exactly like the one that had been parked in front of the Delton Corners ticket booth only a few hours earlier. I laughed a little under my breath. Could it be Ava's? I knew she lived with her parents for the summer, but what were the chances she lived across the street from my summer cabin?

I told the guys I'd see them later and went inside. I made myself a PB and J, scarfed it down while watching Sports Center, and then got in the shower. The hot water felt amazing on my skin.

After the shower I put on a pair of comfy, red mesh shorts and a T-shirt and cracked a beer. I began thinking about radiation again and connected my hotspot so I could search for more information on my tablet. I knew a little about the three types of background radiation humans are exposed to on earth—terrestrial, cosmic, and internal—and spent forty-five minutes reading up on it. When I was finished, I was sure the radiation the CBB was detecting had to be from a space object like a meteor. I made some notes on my tablet to organize my thoughts for when I called Agent Harper the next morning.

I caught sight of the DBT bumper stickers on the cabin wall and felt the urge to see Ava. I frowned and then sighed loudly, disappointed in myself.

With a little reluctance, I emailed a friend at work and asked him to look in the database for Ava's address and phone number. He was a good friend, asking few questions about who she was or why I needed the information.

It was a perfect summer evening, so I grabbed my phone and headed outside to see if anyone was still by the fire. There were a few female Upper Dells guides swinging on an oversized hammock, but most of the crowd had left already. I opened the outer door but let the screen door stay closed. Although it was clean, the cabin still needed a little airing out. I sat down on the step in front of the cabin and checked my phone: *One New Message.*

There it was. Ava's address and phone number. I looked across the street at the green house. It was hers.

Just call her, my heart said.

Don't you dare, my brain replied.

I turned the phone over in my hands a few times. Suzanne's words echoed in my mind. "She's out of your league." And then my mind saw an image of Agent Harper's face in the grass. He wasn't saying anything, but he was staring at me with a stern face. It was a bit disturbing. Suddenly his face blew away like smoke, and Ava walked in through the haze. She was wearing a tight black dress and wore tall black high heels. She flashed a sultry smile and my heart felt like it dropped down to my feet. She washed away with a wave of river water, and then the green grass came back into view.

I stared at the phone for another second.

I took a deep breath. "Screw it," I said aloud and I dialed her number. It rang several times and then went to voicemail.

A red truck pulled into the next street over and stopped in front of Ava's house. I stood up, peering up the alley through the yards. A young guy got out of the truck and walked up to the door. I took a few steps into the alleyway and watched Ava opened the door. The guy looked nervous as hell. And then before I could blink, the dude had climbed the stairs and had Ava in his arms. She struggled to get free, yelling for him to let her go.

"Owe! You're hurting me!" she screamed.

"Dammit! Ava!" I hissed, and bolted across the street.

Chapter Six

I woke up early with work on my mind. I knew Agent Harper was never in the office much before 8:00, so I got up early and went for a three-mile jog while I waited. I ran past Ava's house—no one was awake yet—and through the streets of the neighborhood. I thought about the asshole I pulled off her the night before, and how when I asked her out, she accepted.

I was going on a date with Ava! The thumping of my heart happily drowned out the protests from my brain.

I couldn't hold back a smile as I looped my way down to Broadway. The sidewalks were deserted so early in the morning, and all the shops and restaurants were closed up. The city looked sad without its normal hustle and bustle of tourists crowding the streets. It was nice for a run, though, because there were lots of signs and paraphernalia to look at to help pass the time.

I returned to my cabin sweaty and beat, but at the same time, the spike of adrenaline left me full of energy. I took a long, slow shower and then got dressed. With coffee cup in hand, I read the newspaper out on the camping chair I had set up on my front doorstep. One glance towards Ava's house told me she was at work; her car was not parked out in front anymore. I imagined her standing on the top deck of the *Bailey* looking beautiful and rockin' the microphone.

At 8:30 I decided to hop in the Audi and head out of town to make my work call. I drove down Highway 16 toward Portage and stopped in the parking lot of a drive-in movie theater just out of town. A bright purple ticket booth sat empty to my left. The place was abandoned at this time of day—mine was the only car in the lot. It was perfect.

I got out my cell phone and dialed speed dial number one. An automated voice said, "Classification and identification, please."

"This is agent CBB 65179. Agent Hill calling for Agent Harper, please."

"Cipher accepted. Please hold to be connected."

A new voice came on the line. "Agent Hill, please give the countersign." Harper was double-checking my identity—following protocol.

"Double-stranded nucleotides," I replied.

"Ah, Nolan! How is your placement going? Are you fitting into your temporary Dells life?" I liked Agent Harper. It was rare to find a boss who knew how to employ the perfect amount of both professional and personal interest in his employees.

"It's pretty great, actually. This place is so beautiful." I leaned up against the hood of my shiny, silver Audi.

"Superb. Okay, let me see here..." I could hear him shuffle papers on his desk. "There are some advances in your operation. The techs have narrowed down the location of the source of harmful radiation to two zones. You are still in an active zone and will be asked to remain at your post for the continuation of the cycle or until we apprehend the object. The field agents that were posted in the other zones will be moved to your zone to bulk up protection."

"I see. Sir, I'd like to share some information I think might be useful to this operation." "Go ahead, Agent Hill."

"I have reason to believe the source of radiation is not terrestrial at all, but rather deriving from a cosmic source."

I heard Agent Harper take a deep breath and let it go. "Well, well, Agent Hill. I am impressed. Your next op file was to explain the details of this. Perhaps you'd be better off in intel than out in the field."

Uh-oh. Being stuck behind a desk was not what I wanted to do for the rest of my career. Being out in the field was my passion.

"Oh, well, thank you, sir, but I assure you, the field is where I'm best placed."

"Well, we shall see, won't we?" Then I heard some papers shuffle again. "At any rate, Agent Hill, we have reason to believe that the source of harmful radiation is not lying in a natural position on earth, but we have suspicion that it is being held by an American."

"Interesting," I responded.

"We are unaware if this person is planning to use this source to create a nuclear threat, to build weapons of mass destruction, or simply to try to sell it on the black market for monetary gain. This criminal must be found, and he must be apprehended as soon as possible."

"I understand, sir."

"Actually, you don't quite understand it all yet—there's more. We have reason to believe that the person who has been exposed to this object has been subjected to high levels of dangerous cosmic radiation for several years, and in turn, our geneticists believe this person may be harboring some dangerous mutated genes. We are calling this person 'the Carrier.' The agency is unaware of the effect of these mutated genes on others at this point, but our scientists and geneticists are working hard to create some scenarios."

"Great. Well, I'm glad we are making some progress." I moved my sunglasses down from off of my head and over my eyes. The morning sun stretched across the deserted field.

"Agent Hill, I believe you are one of our most promising agents in the CBB. I assure you, if you carry out this mission and apprehend the Carrier, you will not only be saving America from a certain and imminent disaster, but you will surely be handsomely rewarded within the agency."

"Thank you, sir. I appreciate your confidence in me." How could I respectfully ask my next question? "Sir, I was wondering if I could possibly be privy to a little more information about the Carrier? I don't feel like I fully understand my position as an agent stationed in this area. I want to be as useful as I can, but I'm not sure I know exactly what I am supposed to be doing."

I pictured Agent Harper sitting at his desk looking stylish and professional in his signature black Armani suit. He had a rather large forehead and his blonde hair was cut short to his head and gelled into tiny spikes. His blonde eyebrows were barely seen and reminded me of little cirrus clouds floating over his icy blue eyes. He was a muscular, tall man in his early forties who gave off a vibe that was very serious, but also somewhat approachable at the same time. I waited for Agent Harper's response.

"I admire your dedication to this cause, Nolan. I can also understand your trepidation toward the assignment. I imagine you feel like you're blindly walking down a dark hallway. Let me assure you that you have a purpose at your station. You have been chosen because you fit a profile needed for this operation, and your purpose will become evident to you as time goes on."

It was hard to trust that I was doing my job when I didn't feel like I was doing anything at all, but I said, "I understand. Thank you, sir."

Before Agent Harper hung up, he explained that he would be emailing another set of reports for me to read, and we set up a time for our next call. I stared out over the lonely movie theater for a minute. What was my purpose here? Sit around and wait? For what exactly? A light and refreshing breeze blew across my face as I exhaled heavily. I supposed an answer would become clear soon enough.

I got back in my car thinking, what should I do now? I had almost forgotten. Tonight I had my first date with Ava!

Chapter Seven

The next morning came too early. It wasn't that Ava and I stayed out too late, but rather the fact that once I got home, I was so jacked up from the date that it took me several hours to calm down and then finally fall asleep.

I replayed over and over the perfect night, beginning with when Ava surprised me by introducing me to her mother. Ava's mother was pretty good-looking for a mom with college-aged kids, and her eyes seemed to emit kindness. Maybe Ava was right when she said benevolence ran in her genes.

I thought about my first very important encounter with Ava's mother. I knew the way into a woman's heart had much to do with her mother's and best friend's approval. I had asked if she was enjoying her summer and commented on the book she was reading. I wanted her to feel that Ava was safe with me. Mothers sometimes have a hard time trusting their daughters' boyfriends.

I dragged my ass out of bed and hopped in the shower. I had been looking for a truly authentic Dells date yesterday, and Ava had gotten the job done. I imagined myself standing right next to Ava on top of that towering sandstone cliff overlooking the river again. The Wisconsin River looked more majestic and powerful from our position up above it than it did from down on its surface in a tour boat. The sandstone cliffs that lined its banks were handsomely framing the sparkling water at their feet. It was more gorgeous than anything I had ever seen.

But then I remembered how the setting sun casted soft, yellow glows around Ava's brown hair and sparkled off her face. I decided she looked, without a doubt, just as gorgeous as the scenery.

It was quiet and serene, and it had felt like we were the last two people left on earth.

I turned off the water and grabbed a towel from the rack on the wall.

It honestly was the best date I had ever been on. We had gone through the motions of a typical first date, asking each other questions about family, friends, and our lives up to this point. I had been trained by the FBI to tell part of the truth, but not to blatantly lie. For the first time in my life, I actually wanted to tell the whole truth, but I knew that by not telling Ava, I was protecting her.

I made a couple pieces of peanut butter toast and continued to let my mind wander about last night's events, especially the part when she took me to Make Out Rock, and we, well, made out.

On my way out the door, I poured coffee into my travel mug and then locked up. The whole morning I was thinking about Ava. What she looked like last night, where she took me, what she smelled like, what she sounded like, when I'd see her again... My mind went round and round in circles and, quite frankly, I loved it.

I knew I wouldn't see her today since I was stuck at the Dairy Queen booth all day, and we hadn't made any plans for tonight. It was 8:00 when I parked in the lot. I walked down to the booth, yawning and rubbing my eyes. I should have brought two mugs of coffee. I opened up the door, pulled down the advertisers that were pushed up against the windows, and slid the glass over to open the booth. I was about to sit down on my stool when an extra large tour bus pulled up right in front of my booth and parked there. I was about to leave the booth to explain they couldn't park on the street when the door opened and a mousy, unattractive lady in her thirties got out. She walked over to my window.

"Hi there. I have your 8:30 tour group with Badgerland Tours." She opened up a dark brown folder and tapped her itinerary with her pencil.

This was new to me. "Ah, let me call the office." On the phone, Darren's secretary told me to instruct the tour group how to get down to the Lower Dells Docks since they weren't in the right spot. The lady looked a little ticked when I told her she was in the wrong place.

Just after the huge tour bus left, my phone buzzed with a new text message. It was from Agent Harper.

Check email inbox. New intel on the Carrier.

Activity on the street and sidewalk in front of me was pretty bare, so I decided to read the email from my tablet instead of my phone. I pulled open my CBB-issued briefcase and shuffled through the items inside. The agency had placed me here with plenty of neat gadgets. I found several electronic devices: tiny microphones, bugs, fancy GPS and tracking systems, and night vision goggles sat among other items I was still learning how to use. After a minute I found my tablet near the bottom of the case.

The email was titled "classified" and I had to enter my classification and identification passwords to open it. It was a good-sized email, and I wasn't sure I was awake enough to read something so scientifically wordy and heavy this early in the morning. I rubbed my eye sockets and continued anyway.

New research suggests the source of potentially harmful radiation is from a space object that likely fell onto earth almost a century ago...

"Thank you, Agent Hill," I imitated my boss's voice, "for making this integral discovery."

About an hour after I started my shift, I was buried deep into the science mumbo-jumbo of the report, and barely noticed the big green army Duck pull up in front of the Dairy Queen. It parked there, and then the engine shut off. I looked up and recognized that this Duck was different from the Ducks that go out on tour on the Wisconsin River—this one had stairs built into the side like a bus. I guess they couldn't take those out into the water or they'd end up on the bottom of the river!

A short dude sauntered off the Duck, did a stretch, and gave an obnoxiously loud yawn. The guy caught my eye and came walking over to the booth.

"Hey, buddy! You don't have a coffee maker back there, do ya?" He walked closer and leaned his arm on the counter. This guy was a card.

"Ah, no. Sorry, man."

"Hey, just joshin' ya! I'm Ted. How you doin'?"

"Hey, Ted, I'm Nolan. Nice to meet you." I looked over at the Duck. "What are you doing out here on the street with that big Duck?"

Ted looked confused for a second. He turned around and looked at the Duck behind him and then said, "Oh. You don't know about the shuttle Ducks? The drivers have to take a turn working the shuttle one day a week. We have to drive this big boy downtown, pick up passengers, and take them back to the docks down on Highway 12. We go back and forth all day long."

"Oh. That sucks. Wouldn't you rather be out on the river making money?"

"Exactly. The traffic, the idiots downtown... I do not look forward to Tuesdays."

"Yeah, I bet." Then there was a pause as we both weren't sure what to say next.

"So...is this your first summer working for the boats? I don't think I've seen you around before."

"Yeah. I've only been working a few weeks." I picked up the pen on the counter in front of me and turned it in my hands.

"Oh, hey, you know any tour guides? My good buddy, Ava, works on the Lower Dells."

"Yes, I know Ava!" Then I realized I'd gotten a little too excited at the sound of her name, so I toned it down a little. "Actually, I'm sort of dating her."

"Really? With that hottie?" He was smiling ear to ear.

So it was okay to get excited. "Yeah! She is a really great girl...if you know what I mean."

Ted quickly wiped the smile off his face. "Wait, are you the jerk who threw a punch at my friend Aaron?"

"Oh no, hold on. You've got it all wrong. He was way outta line. Ava was yelling for help."

"Really?" He leaned forward on the counter, looked me straight in the eyes, and lowered his voice. "Ava is a very sweet, perfect girl, and she deserves nothing but the best."

I thought of a conversation Ava and I had last night. "Oh, listen, Ted, I don't think Ava is interested in you. She and I went out last night and she actually told me about your friendship with her. I got the picture she doesn't like you that way."

"Thanks, genius. I figured that out years ago. I was simply trying to give you the gentleman's warning that Ava is a great catch, and I don't want to see her hurt." He gave me the stink eye.

"Gotcha. Good to know." Hurting Ava was not in my plans. Actually, I had no plans at this point. I was a little sick of the lecture from Ted, so I took an interest in the newspaper on the counter.

Ted sensed my dislike in his words. "Listen. I don't know a thing about you..."

"That's right. You don't," I interrupted, probably with more cheek than needed. I don't know why I was feeling so defensive around Ted.

He tried to ignore my rudeness. "But I do know that Ava is a good judge of character. So I'm gonna let you know that Ava is one of my very best friends, and I trust you will be a great friend and...maybe more to her. But, if you lay a hand on her in the wrong way, I will know and I will personally make sure you pay." Then he paused and looked me dead in the eyes and said, "Got it?"

Sure, I punched out his friend, but what made Ted think I would ever hurt Ava? Instead of taking offense from Ted's little lecture, I decided to play the whole thing off as no big deal.

I smiled a little and said, "Got it, Ted. I assure you, I will be nothing but a perfect gentleman to Ava. I know she is something special." Then we shared a moment of understanding. I think Ted saw something in me he didn't before because his face relaxed a bit.

"Alright, buddy. I'm glad we're clear. Now, let's talk business. Did you catch the Brewer's game last night?"

I hadn't caught the baseball game, but I did watch *Sports Center* that morning and was able to hold my own in the baseball conversation. We talked for a few more minutes, and then Ted had some passengers get on his shuttle and he had to take a trip back to the Duck docks.

After he left, I thought a little bit more about Ted, and I hoped Ava knew what a good friend she had. He really was looking out for her own good. I didn't see Ted anymore on the shuttle Duck that day, though. The next time the shuttle showed up, some other guy was driving, and he told me it had got busy, so they had to put Ted on the river. He must have been happy about that.

The morning was moderately busy downtown, and tourists were at my counter all day. I wasn't able to get much reading done, which was slightly annoying, but at the same time, those documents were making me fall asleep. I felt like there was something I was oblivious to, and so the reports didn't make much sense to me. I learn much better audibly than visually, so I figured I would get filled in with Agent Harper's update later.

Chapter Eight

Brian's shift began a few hours after I met Ted. It was an odd shift where the agent came in late to help during the busy time at the Dairy Queen booth, and then mid-afternoon they had to head over to the old, cream-colored, antique Dells Boat Tours building down the street to sell to the dinner cruise crowd.

Brian walked in the door and wasted no time getting to the point. "So, my man. How was the big date last night?"

"Pretty great, buddy, pretty great." The kiss replayed in my mind a few times, and I began feeling a little weak in the knees. I knew my face was giving away my daydream because when I looked over at Brian, he had a huge smile on his face as if he could see the same movie I had playing in my head.

"Ah, I've seen that look before. You really like this girl, don't you?" Brian punched me playfully in the shoulder.

I wished I could wipe that stupid smile off my face, as I was sure I looked like a gleaming idiot, but the corners of my mouth wouldn't turn down. "You know, Brian, I haven't felt like this in a really, really long time. She just...does something to me, you know?"

You're in trouble, my brain warned.

"I know, I know, my friend. I've been there before." He waited a few seconds, and I could tell he was recalling some old memories. Then his face turned hard. "She broke my heart...but hey, I'm sure that won't happen to you."

Brian too? Jeez, did every eligible guy who walked through Ava's path try to win her heart?

I thought for a second about how this new relationship might end, but I couldn't imagine. Or was it that I didn't want to imagine it?

"She is a pretty special woman, Nolan. Just know that." Brian looked pretty serious. This was the second warning of the day about treating Ava the right way. I wasn't sure how to take it. Did I come off as a complete jerk to everyone who barely knew me?

"Don't think I don't know that, Brian. I agree completely with you!"

An elderly couple stepped up to the ticket window, cutting off our conversation. The subject of dating Ava didn't come up anymore in the day's conversations, and for me, the shift flew by mostly because of Brian.

Before I knew it, it was time for Brian to head over to the other booth, leaving me to people-watch and read the newspaper. Late in the day I caught myself checking my till and counting my tickets. I hadn't sold too many today and my instant reaction was disappointment.

"Nolan. This job is only a cover," I said to myself.

Maybe I was getting in too deep.

My phone buzzed with a new message from the CBB. The text was requiring me to become familiar with several new apps that had been uploaded to my phone and tablet. There was a new search engine for FBI databases, a series of maps with several different overlays, a bio scanner with a night feature, and a Geiger counter suitable for searching out cosmic radiation.

Ah-ha. Tools that could be useful.

I spent the next hour studying the maps and learning how to use the Geiger counter.

I packed up after Ava and Ted surprised me with a visit to my booth, and I left them eating ice cream together at the neighboring Dairy Queen. I turned my Audi left out of the parking lot and headed north of town on a mission.

I followed Highway 13 to a Wayside Park on the edge of the city of Wisconsin Dells. The small park was empty as I pulled into one of the five parking stalls available. A sign reading *restrooms* in yellow lettering was nailed to a dark-brown, small log cabin just off the parking lot. It looked like the kind of place where the toilet was simply a board with a hole in it over a pit in the ground. No thanks. I'd rather crap in the woods.

I shifted the car into park and took out my tablet, opening the Geiger counter app. I wasn't sure how well it would work, but I began to scan the area. In seconds a report spit out the amount of radiation in the immediate three-hundred-foot radius. The numbers were low. Incredibly low.

I smiled. It worked.

I frowned. This would take forever. I had to scan the entire city in three-hundred-foot sections. But then again, I sort of wanted it to take forever.

*   *   *   *

I scanned seven more times on my way back down Highway 13 and back into the city. Most of the readings were the same as the first, with the exception of the last, which showed slightly higher numbers. I felt hopeful that I might be able to find the source of the radiation after all.

There was a party flaring up at Animal Island as I returned to my tiny summer cabin, and I decided to indulge for a while. I was happy to meet a few more employees, and I spent a lot of time talking to a pair of guys who lived in the Ukraine. They came over for the summer to make some money for their families back home. They were very funny and very willing to share their life stories with me. I found it all very interesting.

I tried to prevent it, but I kept looking over at Ava's house, checking for Ava's Olds. It hadn't showed up yet. What could she be doing with Ted that long? They had ice cream hours ago.

I suddenly experienced a pang of panic and wanted to call her and check if she was okay. No, that's stupid. Of course she was okay. She was a grown woman and could take care of herself. Except for the time she almost tumbled down the hill, and when she almost got molested by her ex.

Nerves rumbled in my stomach. Calling her would definitely come off as overprotective and annoying. I tried to ignore the nerves, but they persisted. I craved Ava by my side and felt uneasy not knowing what she was doing. As if someone slapped me in the side of my face, I stood abruptly from the fire and shook my whole body. How had I developed such strong feelings for Ava so quickly?

It was almost midnight, and although the party was still rollin', I decided to call it a night. Just as I opened the screen door to my cabin, I saw headlights one street over. It was Ava. She got out of the car alone, walked inside, and turned the front porch light off. She never even looked over at Animal Island.

The sinking feeling returned to my body. Maybe I was in this relationship deeper than Ava was.

Chapter Nine

The next day I knew I had to step up my game a little. I stopped at the florist on my way to work and bought a dozen red roses and a blank card. On my way in I noticed that Brian was alone at Lower One. It was too early for Suzanne's shift to start—perfect.

"Hey, Brian! How's it goin', buddy"? I walked up to the booth and went in the door. "I was wondering if you'd do me a favor? You know I've got my eye on Ava, and I think I need to do something romantic to sort of reel her in. Would you help me pull something off?"

"Oh, God. I don't have to sing or dance or something embarrassing like that, right?" Brian said.

"No, no, buddy, nothing like that. I bought some flowers and a note, and I stuck it on her windshield." I pointed out the ticket window. "I'm sure she's going to come up here to Lower One to hang out after one of her first trips, and I need you to tell her to go look at her car." I gave him a manly pat on the back.

"Right, right. I can do that. No prob." A couple came up to the window to buy some tickets, so I snuck out the door and headed back to Lower Two.

Once the booth was open, I took a seat, sat back, and watched the Bailey come into the bay to dock. Less than twenty passengers shuffled off the boat, and then Jack and Ava walked up the stairs together. She looked so good in her uniform, and I loved seeing her laugh and smile—it simply lit up her eyes.

At the top of the stairs, they split up. Jack headed straight for the Last Chance snack shop, and Ava bolted it over to the bathroom. A few customers approached my window, and I kept busy for almost twenty minutes. Ava never stopped by, and a small feeling of frustration filled my heart when I realized she had decided to go to Lower One instead of my booth. I thought for sure she'd come see me before she went to say hi to Brian.

Well good, then Brian would tell her to look at her car, and she'd see the roses and come running back to my booth.

More customers came, more minutes passed, but still no Ava. Nerves brewed in my stomach and my heart sank. Maybe I had made a big mistake. It was entirely possible that she didn't think about me every second they way I thought about her.

For a moment I considered running out to Ava's car and whisking the roses off the windshield before Brian told her about it, but I abandoned the idea. I tried to replay our date in my mind to see if I could recall any sign that she wasn't enjoying herself, that I had done something wrong. But my mind was only filled with her smiling face and our sweet kisses.

I took a deep breath and told myself to trust my first instinct.

I glanced towards the front ticket booth and there she was, walking casually back through the waiting area with Jack. I looked carefully—no flowers or card in her hand!

My momentary excitement crashed down to the ground. Had she thrown them away?

This was not good.

Ava and Jack loaded up their boat and then headed back downriver for another tour.

Crap! This was not working out as I thought it would.

I picked up the phone and called the front booth, but no one answered so I couldn't get the scoop from Brian. I let out a sigh. Ava would be back in only one hour. I'd have to wait to see whether she got my note and the flowers.

I pulled out my tablet and tried to read the reports Agent Harper had emailed me. My eyes kept darting toward the window facing the river, subconsciously wondering where Ava was. Customers came and went. One hour started to feel like five. But then I saw it: the blue and white tour boat coming around the bend. It pulled into the dock and several people got off. Ava and Jack walked up the stairs and split up again. This time Jack went towards Lower One and Ava was walking towards my booth. My heart turned flips inside my rib cage. My stomach was suddenly infested with fluttery butterflies! I quickly turned away and looked out the front window as she approached the booth.

Play it cool, kid.

The door opened and I turned to see pretty Ava as she graced me with her presence.

I couldn't hide my smile. I carefully read her face, especially those beautiful brown eyes, for any hint that she was happy to see me. I dared to tell her I was glad to see her, although if my heart had a microphone it would certainly be saying a lot more.

"It's great to see you, too." She smiled sweetly at me and then took a seat.

It was a good sign. The butterflies kept fluttering, but backed down a bit.

"Did you and Ted have a nice time last night?"

Wait, stop...don't go there! Keep it about you and her!

I watched her lips move as she talked about her evening. Her whole face was sparkling. Her mouth was moving, but I was having trouble focusing on her words until I heard her say, "I told him a lot about you."

"Really? All good, I hope."

"Absolutely. I didn't have a bad word to say."

Ah-ha.

The butterflies subsided some more. Should I say something about the roses? What if Brian hadn't said anything to her yet? I didn't want to ruin the surprise, so I decided to let it wait a little longer and see what panned out.

A few groups of customers showed up at my window, and Ava and I chatted a bit between sales. We had a nice little visit together until she had to leave for her next trip. I didn't want to let her go without a little something for her to daydream about, so when she hopped off her stool, I took a risk. Moving in close, I put my hand on her lower back and stuck my cheek right next to hers. I inhaled the sweet scent of her hair and knew she'd smell my cologne. I pulled back, slowly brushing my cheek across hers and then kissed her lips quickly. "Have a great trip," I whispered in her ear, and hopefully she left with her head spinning exactly like mine was.

The day slugged by slowly, mostly because Ava only came to see me once more. If she was playing hard-to-get, then she was damn good at it because her two visits only made me crave her more. Late in the afternoon, I noticed Jack loading up the Bailey, but Ava wasn't on the dock with him. I stared down at the dock confused for a while, until I saw Ava running madly through the waiting area. In her left hand she carried a bouquet of very wilted and ugly roses.

Dammit, Brian! Last time I ask him for a favor.

I had the early shift and it ended while Ava was still out on her tour. I closed up the booth and walked out to my car. Suzanne was the only one at Lower One, and I didn't feel like talking to her, so I pretended I was on my phone as I walked by the booth. She waved, and I gave her a nod.

There were a few hours before my date with Ava would begin, should she accept it, so I headed south of town on Highway 16 to do some more scanning with my Geiger counter app. I took eleven scans, recording each reading in a document, and ended up only a few blocks from Animal Island. I drove back to my cabin and changed out of my boat uniform before checking over the data I had collected.

Just as before, the readings became stronger as I headed towards the center of the city. This was good news;

I felt productive. I thought about heading out to take some more readings, but there were only twenty minutes before Ava may appear for our date.

Anticipation and eagerness were taking over my body as I got ready. I guess that was good, though, because those feelings made me want to clean up a bit. I picked up the dirty clothes off the floor, put the food wrappers in the garbage, and even wiped down the toilet and sink. Then I made the bed and shoved my CBB briefcase under it. I wasn't expecting the date to end up in the cabin, but I wanted to be ready, just the same.

Chapter Ten

As 7:15 rolled around, I heard people out at the campfire. I thought I might as well go socialize while I waited for the hands of the clock to swing around, so I dressed in my favorite plaid golf shorts and a plain white T-shirt, spritzed on some cologne, and headed out the door. Almost all the boat employees that lived at Animal Island were out. They had music pumping, and the bonfire was roaring. I talked with a few guys I had never met before and then chatted with the Ukrainians again. God, they were funny. I wondered what Ava was doing and often looked back at her house, waiting for a precious glimpse of her.

Right before 8:00, an Upper Dells pilot, who was very short but full of spunk, yelled to the crowd that he had decided to move the party to the docks and take a boat upriver. Within minutes, the party dispersed, and I found myself left alone with a few Upper Dells female guides I didn't know very well.

"Hey Nolan, you should come out with us tonight," one of the guides said. "We're gonna head downtown to the bars. Wanna come?" She looked about eighteen and had long, curly red hair. I was not attracted to her in the slightest, but I could tell by the way she was looking at me that she was trying to hit on me.

Good luck.

"No thanks, ladies. I've got plans tonight." I had passed on a few beers during the party because I didn't want to smell like I had been drinking when Ava and I went out. I took a sip on the water bottle someone had offered me instead.

"Awww...come on Nolan. We'll keep you company all night long!" The other guide, who was equally unattractive to me (okay, she was downright ugly), tried to move over closer and touched my upper thigh. I jumped up quickly and told them I had forgotten something inside. I ran into my cabin and then peeked out the window through the closed shades. The girls stood up, got in their car, and left.

Thank God. I'd have to remember to avoid them from now on.

Once everyone left I went back outside, locked the door to my cabin, and then took a seat by the roaring fire. I stared into the flames, letting the sight take me away with my thoughts. I thought about how much I liked Ava, about my undercover job with the CBB, and about the mysterious Carrier whom I was supposed to apprehend. I pulled out my phone and went over the data I had collected with my new apps. The numbers got larger as I entered the heart of the city.

"It's near the middle of town," I said out loud. Although it went against the process I had organized, I decided to do a scan right there on Animal Island. I stood up and ran the app, holding my phone flat out in front of me. It finished scanning with a loud beep.

I gasped—the reading was through the roof.

"This has to be a mistake," I said as I ran the app again. A few seconds later the scan completed and the number was the same. My jaw dropped. It was like I was standing right next to a huge meteor. I turned a slow circle, heart beating out of control, looking for the gigantic space rock that must be sitting in a pile of grass right outside my cabin. But instead I turned to see Ava walking down the alley towards me. My mouth involuntarily spilled out what my mind was thinking. "You look absolutely beautiful."

I pocketed my phone. *No! You're onto something!* my brain urged.

But I saw sorrow in Ava's eyes and my heart took precedence. She hadn't smiled yet. "What's wrong?" I asked carefully.

She was reluctant to tell me. Was it about me? I couldn't play it off like there was nothing wrong. I had to make her comfortable enough to tell me what was bothering her. I asked her to sit next to me and gently put my hand around her back and kissed her sweet face.

I had never seen her like this before.

Finally she showed me an email from her college. She was on academic probation. My heart broke for her as I watched tears form in her eyes. I felt so sorry for her. She wanted nothing more than to be a teacher, but her freshman year had been somewhat of a disaster.

My mind raced back to the time I punched Aaron in the face. Was he to blame for this?

I tried my best to make her feel better and finally a beautiful smiled showed on her lips. She was going to be okay.

We took a quick tour of my cabin and then my phone buzzed in my pocket as I had opened the car door for Ava. With my back turned to the window, I pulled it out—a new text from Agent Harper. I looked over my shoulder inside the window and saw Ava touching the dials on the dashboard, so I clicked to retrieve my message.

New intel acquired. Report by phone, 7:30am.

Interesting. What could the new intel be? I put the phone back in my pocket and pulled open the door. When I sat down I leaned over and put an open hand on the console, hoping she'd take the hint and make a move.

Ava was impressed with the Audi and placed her hand on my arm, her thumb rubbing my skin very sweetly as she gushed about the car. I moved my arm so I could hold her hand in mine. It was very soft and comfortable.

Just as I began to fly high with the excitement of a new relationship, my brain interrupted with a nervous thought—*You shouldn't be starting a relationship, considering the secrets and lies it will have to endure.*

Then, as if she knew I needed to hear it, Ava told me how much she enjoyed being in my company. And with those few words, all my insecurities and worries melted away. If it felt wonderful simply being with Ava, then it was the right choice. At least for now.

Chapter Eleven

The next morning, my cell phone alarm went off at seven. I lay in bed staring at the ceiling for a few minutes, replaying every sweet minute I had spent with Ava the night before. I knew I had to get up and going in order to find a secure place to make the phone call to the CBB, but had trouble convincing myself to pull the blankets back. I was actually feeling a little anxious about the call. I hadn't found enough focus to read the reports from Agent Harper before my date, and when I got home, I collapsed into bed, Ava filling my dreams all night.

I grabbed my CBB briefcase, threw on some clothes, and headed out to my car. Nothing was stirring so early at Animal Island.

I drove out to the same drive-in movie theater I had last week and parked in the lot again. I looked at my phone—7:28. I dialed the number for the CBB and heard the familiar voice asking for my identification and classification. Soon Agent Harper was on the phone, and he got right down to business.

"I have some exciting news for you, Nolan. I've been cleared to disclose to you the latest intelligence acquired by our techs. I assume you've read the email documents I sent you?"

Crap!

"Well, actually, I'm not quite all the way through them yet."

I quickly rifled through my briefcase until I found the tablet and started looking through the reports as he was talking.

"Disappointing, Agent Hill. I assume you will make it a priority today to finish reading the reports?"

"Yes, sir. I will."

How the hell was I going to do that? I had planned to spend the day with Ava.

"Let me give you a synopsis. As you know, the CBB has been aware for quite some time of a complicated public health and safety risk. The problem is the geneticists are unsure just how this conundrum will exactly affect the public. It could be very minor, or it could turn into mass hysteria. Our job is to keep the public free from this knowledge until the risk has been destroyed. Secrecy is a top priority."

"Absolutely." I was good at keeping secrets.

"The CBB has been eliciting extremely high and unusual readings of gamma radiation from the tri-state area. Although gamma radiation is easily detected by survey meters with a sodium iodide detector probe, our scientists are having trouble discerning the most dangerous source of radiation since multiple types of radiation are ubiquitous. There are many kinds of radiation floating through our atmosphere everyday. The major source of this penetrating radiation must be found as quickly as possible before the public is exposed to levels that could cause devastating health problems." "How difficult will it be to find the actual source of radiation?"

"Harder than you think. It most likely looks like a regular run-of-the-mill gemstone. Our scientists believe the radiation from this rock could be harnessed and turned into some kind of next generation bomb. Although we have to be aware of the possibility that someone has simply picked it up and keeps it in their house as a keepsake, it is more likely that the person carrying the item is fully aware of its dangerous and criminally useful nature. "

Ah, the Carrier. Things are starting to make a little more sense.

"Sir, I've been using the Geiger counter app you've sent to my equipment. I think I've found an area with higher levels of radiation." This stuff was getting my blood pumping. I was excited to be a field agent and put to use the months and months of training I've endured.

"I'm happy you've been actively engaged in this mission, Agent Hill, but those apps can be somewhat unreliable. They're all lite versions of more sophisticated equipment we're developing in the labs. Either way, please email me your findings and I'll have tech take a look at it."

Unreliable? Maybe that's why I couldn't see the meteor when I had such a high reading.

"The CBB techs are still working hard to pinpoint the exact location, using our state-of-the-art instruments, and now we believe the item is within a hundred-mile radius of Wisconsin Dells. We want you to keep your eyes and ears open to see if you can get some insider information from the locals in town. Once the CBB has found the exact point of radiation, we will need your help to apprehend the item as well as the person who has been hiding this dangerous rock."

Exciting.

"I understand, Agent Harper. Thank you for the report. I will let you know if I hear any rumbles around town."

Agent Harper thanked me and hung up without setting up another phone meeting time. It was only 7:50, so I stayed at the drive-in for a while longer and read the email documents. For the first time I felt like a real FBI agent. Excitement flowed quickly through my veins as I focused on my reading.

The documents were basically textbook pages of information about the awful health hazards related to exposure to this type of radiation, ranging from radiation sickness, cell death, and DNA damage.

When I was finished, I realized I had spent about forty-five minutes and hadn't once thought about Ava. This was the first time in a few days that Ava hadn't consumed my every moment.

This is what you're meant to do, my brain explained. *Your job is just as thrilling as some potential relationship with Ava.*

But somehow the passion I felt when I was with Ava was completely different from the excitement I experienced when immersed in agency work.

I thought I should do some more scanning, even though Agent Harper thought the app was useless. It would be so much more convenient if I could scan a larger area at once, or get to some parts of town that weren't very accessible by roads.

Just as this thought crossed my mind, I heard a helicopter overhead and got an idea—I could take Ava up in a romantic helicopter ride, and really scan the whole area from up in the sky!

"Nolan, you're a genius!" I said to myself.

I searched the Internet on my phone and found the phone number to the helicopter rides in town. I made a reservation for two for 10:30. Although I had a mild fear of heights, I knew they didn't bother Ava after she pulled me so close to the edge of Make Out Rock. I'd have to suck it up for the short ride. I stopped off at the local market on my way home to pick up a few items for a surprise beach picnic.

* * * *

Later that evening I decided to stop daydreaming about the amazing day I had had with Ava and do some CBB work. The lock on my briefcase had become sticky lately and it took me almost five minutes and much frustration to get it to open. I decided to disconnect the security keypad for the time being. Was someone going to try to break into my tiny cabin in the middle of tourist-town USA and steal my CBB issued tech items? I think not.

I pulled out my tablet and sat on the couch analyzing the results of the scan I had taken on the helicopter. It was still hard to believe I scanned the entire city from the air without Ava knowing what I was up to!

The ride was amazing, though, and it was so fun to see Ava so elated.

I used my tablet to merge the data I had collected into another app that drew a map of the Wisconsin Dells area and overlaid colors corresponding with the readings of radiation I had taken. There were three areas where high levels of radiation were present: one north of town on Stand Rock Road, one on the outskirts of the Oak Lawn subdivision, and the last being a four-block range right over Animal Island.

"The app is somewhat unreliable," I heard Agent Harper's voice say in my ear. But what was the harm in investigating the areas showing higher radiation?

I glanced at the date on my computer. It was almost the Fourth of July. This summer was slipping by me. Harper's message began to occupy my thoughts. What if I'm leaving the Dells soon? What if we apprehend the Carrier before the Fourth of July? What about Ava?

My brain's logic echoed in my mind. *You were a fool to fall for her. Your relationship can only end in heartache.*

I wanted so badly to tell Ava the truth about my job at the CBB and why I was in the Dells, but I knew that could potentially put her in danger. My heart was screaming at my brain. *Live in the moment and enjoy each second you spend with her, even if in the end you suffer.*

I thought back to the walk we took through the prairie before we made out in the cave off of the beach. Ava had been asking some probing questions, looking for some serious information about who I was and what my life's aspirations were. I panicked, and spewed some junk about the Peace Corps. I was cooking up some crap, and I could tell she smelled it.

What are you going to do, Nolan? I had thought in the moment. *Break it off before she's too committed.*

I pushed my brain's challenge out of my mind. No matter how illogical it was, I wanted to be with Ava. There had to be a way to continue my mission and date Ava at the same time, I knew it. And that's exactly what I intended to do.

Chapter Twelve

The next day I had a late shift at work, so I woke up early and drove down Stand Rock road to check out the high radiation levels I had found when I scanned the city from the helicopter. The map I created of the city showed a high reading at KOA Campground one mile from downtown. The grounds were well kept and full of flower beds, waterfalls, and places to relax. I drove straight past the tiny log cabins that lined the driveway under tall pine trees and parked my car in front of the office building.

I had called ahead and made an appointment to meet with Hayward Kubas, the manager and owner of the property. Just as I shut off the ignition, the office door opened and an overweight older man wearing jean overalls and a red flannel shirt shuffled out. He waved at me and yelled a greeting as I got out of the car.

"Hello there! Mr. Nolan, right?" He took a few slow steps down the ramp in front of the office and waved a hand in the air at me. "I can tell it's you from yer fancy car." He spoke with a slight old-timey feel.

"Good morning, Mr. Kubas."

"Call me Hayward, son!" he held out a hand to welcome me in. "Come on in. I've got the coffee brewin'!"

"Thank you, sir." I followed the large man up the ramp, taking advantage of the extra-slow-Hayward-pace to scan the area as I waited. No obvious meteors.

The office was outdated, but cozy. Hayward shuffled behind his wooden desk and offered me a seat in a 1970s green velour high-armed swivel chair. He poured two mugs of black coffee and took a long sip before offering me one.

"What can I do for ya, Mr. Nolan?" Hayward's chin had stubbly, grey hairs and his eyes were a calm, pale green.

"I'm a local scientist and..."

"Science?" he interrupted, thumping his hand down on the desk. "What sort of science?" He leaned forward with big eyes, looking slightly like an overexcited bear.

"Well I'm a student of all sciences, actually, but I'm most interested in astronomy these days."

"Astronomy," Hayward repeated dreamily. "Like outer space and junk?"

I chuckled a little. "Yes, exactly."

"Oh, I love space. If I hadn't inherited this place from my parents forty-five years ago, I would have gone off to college and learned about them alien life forms."

"So you've lived here all your life, Hayward?"

"Oh yes, quite so. My family tree goes way back to the times when the Ho-Chunk walked through these forests."

"Amazing. Look, I'm searching for places around the area that may have been hit by recent meteor showers. Have you heard of any such instances while you or your family have been around here?"

Hayward scrunched up his forehead and itched the back of his head. "Well, nothing out of the ordinary, I don't suppose."

"I see," I said, disappointed.

Hayward stuck his pointer finger up in the air. "Well, unless you count the great meteor shower of 1913!"

Good grief.

"Yes, that's exactly the sort of thing I'm looking for! What can you tell me about it?" I took out my tablet and opened a new document, ready to take notes.

"My grandfather used to tell stories of the night when bright blue rocks radiating tall flames of purple fire fell from the sky."

"Blue rocks? Purple fire?" Perhaps Hayward was as crazy as they came. I wrote down a note and then closed my tablet's screen.

"Yes sir. Sure as the moon itself. Blue rocks licked with purple fire fell from the night sky."

"Very interesting. Did you grandfather keep one of these blueish purple fire rocks?"

"No, sir, Mr. Nolan, he did not. Scared to death of it, you know. Thought it was from the devil himself. The blue devil, of course."

"Right..." I took a sip from the mug in front of me and just about choked. It tasted like something that dripped from the underside of my car. I set the mug back down quickly. "How about recently, Hayward. Have you noticed any blue or other colored rocks falling from the sky anytime since you've been here?"

"Naw. I haven't been lucky enough to witness that kinda miracle." He took a long sip of his coffee and then muttered, "Shoulda gone to college."

A loud knock rapped on the door of the office.

"Come in," Hayward yelled.

A very short woman, probably about five feet tall, entered the room. "Hay, the bus of girl scouts has arrived. Come on out to greet 'em!"

"Yes, ma'am," he called back. Then he leaned across the desk and held out his hand for a shake. "Well, I've gotta go, Mr. Nolan. It's been a pleasure."

"Same here, Hayward. Say, would you mind if I took a look around? Your grounds are beautiful."

"Be my guest, son!" Then he lifted one eyebrow. "But watch out for them devilish blue rocks."

I snickered and he responded with a very loud belly laugh. I followed Hayward out of the building and took a sharp left at the bottom of the ramp, heading towards the RV camping sites. I retrieved my phone from my pocket and checked the time. I had one hour before my shift began at Lower Two. I turned on the Geiger counter app and strolled through the campgrounds, watching the numbers. They were highest at the very back of the campground and soon I found myself standing at a high chain-link fence staring into a hazardous waste dump site.

"Well, there's the source of radiation. Nothing cosmic about this junk."

I headed back through the campground with my eyes pasted to my cell app. The numbers continued to decline as I reached Hayward's office. I dejectedly opened my car door and slid into the driver's seat. I had secretly wished this was the answer. That Hayward had a meteor sitting on a pedestal at the entrance gates for all to see as they entered the campgrounds.

Oh well. One dead end wasn't going to stop me. I had two more areas of high radiation to check out. If only I could investigate them immediately instead of heading off to my fake job. But I smiled as I pulled back onto Stand Rock road—I'd be seeing my Ava within a few minutes.

* * * *

I had full shifts at DBT for the next few days and spent any free time I had with Ava. I didn't get back to my investigation for the CBB until three days later when I had my next day off. Ava was scheduled to work, so I took advantage of my time alone.

The campground had been a bust, and I was hoping one of the last two areas would be what the CBB was looking for. I began with the subdivision east of town called Oak Lawn. I turned down Webber Avenue into the middle of the subdivision. I passed many newer houses, many of them much larger than the ones in Ava's neighborhood. I took Webber all the way until it met Pleasant View Drive, which ran along the back of the subdivision. There I parked my Audi on the quiet street and took out my tablet. I ran the Geiger counter app and got to work. It took a while, but I continued to scan until the numbers began to rise, just like at the campground.

I found myself at a new construction site on the far north side of the neighborhood. Crews were busy pouring a foundation for a house and excavating the land with backhoes. I parked and took a scan with my app.

It had the highest reading I had taken that day.

I spotted the site foreman and approached him.

"This is a hard hat area only, buddy," he yelled over the machines' noise. "You've got to go."

"I'm Stan from the Nuclear Regulatory Commission investigating a high radiation scan of this area."

"The NRC?" he said, guiding me out to the street and away from the machinery. "The high radiation must be the radon. Almost every house in this neighborhood has to install a mitigation system to get the radon out of their houses." He waved a hand behind him. "This place is loaded with it!"

"High radon levels in the soil, huh?"

Dammit. This can't be the source.

"Yep."

"Well, thank you. I will report back to my office with this information." I began to walk away towards my car and the foreman yelled across the street to me, "The NRC already knows! I'm not sure why they sent you!"

I shut the car door and nodded politely while I drove off.

Last stop—Ava's neighborhood.

Scanning the area around Animal Island was not as easy as the campground or subdivision. I could tell the numbers were higher, but it was hard to pinpoint a specific location of any kind. When I wasn't with Ava I had knocked on a few doors, asking local residents questions that might lead me to the source, but no one seemed to know much about radiation in the area. I had spent much of my free time wandering through the streets surrounding

Animal Island, but there was nothing out of the ordinary that could indicate a reason for higher radiation. Nothing I could see, anyway.

My lite little app wasn't doing the trick. I needed the CBB to bring in the heavy equipment. But the reality of what I was doing began to set in—I would be moved to another location once I located the exact source of harmful radiation and the CBB apprehended the Carrier. By fulfilling all my job requirements I was essentially ending my relationship with Ava. So what if I bought myself some time by not reporting my findings to Agent Harper immediately after I'd uncovered them?

I had told Ava I loved her on the Fourth of July, but I was sure she didn't hear me over the fireworks' booms. I hadn't found the guts to tell Ava again that I loved her. I couldn't ever find the right time, and quite frankly I was scared. I knew we had both invested nearly the entire summer—and, at least for me, almost all of my heart—to each other. As much as I tried, I couldn't think of a scenario where our relationship would end happily. Every time thoughts of what was going to happen to us jumped into my head, I pushed them out. A gutless way to deal with life, I knew, but it was too painful to confront reality—the end of summer probably meant the end of our relationship.

Chapter Thirteen

Soon August was in full swing and one day came the worst day of my life. I woke up that morning and realized that in less than a week, Ava would have to return to college, and I needed to make something happen regarding our relationship. Either I cut her loose or find a way that we could be together.

I was getting ready for work when I heard a knock on the cabin door. My heart skipped a beat—maybe Ava came to say good morning to me before she had to head off to work. When I opened the door, my heart fell right out of my chest. Standing in the doorway, dressed in his perfectly ironed, black Armani suit, was Agent Harper. His blonde hair was cropped perfectly, and he was wearing black Versace sunglasses. "Agent Hill, the day has come. The CBB is in desperate need of your help."

He plowed right through the door into the cabin before I could say anything in response. I noticed a few Upper Dells guides peering out of their cabins across the way with strange looks on their faces. I shut the door quickly and then pulled the blinds down over the front window. When I turned around, Agent Harper looked bothered.

"Sorry, kid, this place is disgusting. I guess you'll be happy when the day is done. We'll soon apprehend the Carrier, and you'll get to move back into your apartment in

Chicago." He picked up a dirty sock from the couch and threw it on the floor. Then he carefully took a seat.

My knees lost their hold, and I involuntarily slid onto the bed.

Today? No. No!

My insides were twisting. I had been pushing this out of my mind for the last few weeks. I was not ready for this. Poor Ava. I hadn't prepared her at all for the end of our relationship. What was I thinking by avoiding the topic?

"Agent Hill, are you feeling alright? You look pale. Do you need to grab a bite to eat before I give you the protocol?"

My gaze moved up from the floor to Agent Harper's face. Eating was the last thing I should be doing. I managed to reply, "No, sir. I'll be alright. Please continue."

"Fine. Today's mission is two-fold. Part one is to locate and destroy the space object that is emitting dangerous radiation. Your work has narrowed it down considerably."

What? But I haven't shared that info with the CBB.

"We've just about locked in our coordinates. Our techs have discovered that we must carry out this mission before the sun sets at nine o'clock tonight.

"Our scientists have been building computer models to project the nuclear decay in similar parent isotopes, considering physical and chemical conditions that may have occurred at different time periods—I know, next generation stuff, right?—and they have come to the conclusion with much certainty that the item is at risk to blow up. What's more, our research has finally pointed to today's date, indicating that the meteor will likely detonate not unlike a nuclear bomb. If we allow this to happen, not only all of Wisconsin but much of the Midwest will be destroyed. Mass panic and chaos will likely ensue. Blackouts, fires, raids, and terror of all kinds will strike the people of this area who were not blasted to char."

If this dangerous object was somewhere in the neighborhood, as I suspected, and I didn't assist in destroying this object, there would be little chance that Ava and I would survive anyway. "Sounds like an important mission. What is part two?" I asked, trying to hide my nerves.

"Part two involves us bringing down the citizen who has harbored this object and willingly endangered the citizens of Wisconsin and of the United States. The Carrier has been exposed to this object for possibly the past twenty years. As I'm sure you've read in the reports, our geneticists have determined that the specific type of radiation from this rock negatively affects human DNA and brain activity. It slowly mutates the neurons that control brain activity, specifically in the hypothalamus and amygdala. As I am sure you know, Agent Hill, these areas control emotions, memory, and fear. Intense aggressive and fierce violent tendencies increase two-fold through each generation of genes exposed to the radiation. If the object has been passed down as an heirloom, as we suspect, then the current Carrier is now the fourth generation vulnerable to this dangerous object.

"It has taken CBB ten years to learn enough about this type of radiation, as it is very rare. What's more, our scientists and research team have discovered that the radiation enters the body and then lays dormant for almost twenty years. The victims don't even know that their DNA is under attack. After those twenty years, the mutated genes become actively aggressive and quickly take over the brain. At that point, there will be no stopping this monster. The Carrier must be destroyed upon discovery."

This was all very odd. I couldn't believe he was actually telling me the truth, but suddenly my mind raced back to that first night I was inside Ava's house, and I followed her up to her bedroom. I had noticed something strange sitting on the bookshelf by the door. An odd, bluish rock sat under a glass dome and was obviously on display.

I heard Hayward's voice in my head: "A blue rock fell from the sky."

Could she possibly be?

Agent Harper knew I had realized the secret. "Yes, Agent Hill. Ava Gardner is the Carrier, and we believe her family is involved as well."

My mouth dropped open, but I had no voice. I bent over for my stomach to retch, but nothing came up. I fell to my knees and gasped for breath. This couldn't be happening.

My Ava. My sweet, sweet Ava. There was no way she was the Carrier.

"But how?" I muttered.

Agent Harper rose from the couch and pulled me up from the ground fiercely by the arm. "Get up!" he yelled, suddenly angry. "You've been bugged—your cabin, your car, your ticket booth, even your damn shoes! We know exactly where you've been and who you've talked to. We've downloaded every text, every call, and every app you've run on your phone. We've been following you all summer, Agent Hill. We know you have a relationship with this woman. *You* helped us into that house. *You* got the family history we needed. It was so perfect I couldn't have planned it better."

I stared at him through raging eyes.

"If you'd like to stay with the agency, it needs to be you who kills her. I told you that you would be very integral in carrying out the CBB's objectives. You will get her alone and do the job quickly and quietly."

"NO!" I screamed at the top of my lungs. I was suddenly angry at myself. I had let my feelings get in the way of my work and now I was in a dreadful situation.

"She doesn't have to die!" There had to be a logical solution. "We can take her to CBB. The geniuses over there can fix her up." I pleaded with Agent Harper. "She won't be twenty for two more weeks..."

Agent Harper cut me off. "No, Agent Hill, Miss Gardner is not a project to be fixed. We cannot put tens of thousands of people at risk just so your pretty little lover can become a genetic experiment. She is a federal criminal!"

"Absolutely not!" I tried to control my breathing. "I am confident that Ava has no idea the implications of this rock. She just thinks it's pretty."

Agent Harper laughed maniacally. "Oh, Agent Hill, you are so naive. Ava Gardner and her family know exactly what they are doing. She and her family need to be destroyed."

That couldn't be true. I spent the entire summer with her. She gave me no reason to believe she was a hardened criminal. The thought was preposterous!

"I won't do it!" I screamed from deep within me. I turned to grab my keys off the side table. I was going to find Ava and then get the hell out of here, but Agent Harper slapped my cheek hard and then grabbed my neck, pushing me up against the wall. Everything on the table came crashing down.

He got within inches of my nose and said in a threatening but steady voice, "You *will* go sell tour tickets today." He paused and then continued. "You *will* act normal. You *will* convince Ms. Gardner to come to your cabin tonight. And as other agents are securing the meteor, you *will* destroy the Carrier. If you don't, I will personally exterminate you *and* your disgusting little criminal girlfriend. Got it, kid?"

I wanted to wipe his spit from my face, but my arms were pinned down. His eyes stared deeply into mine, and I felt a fire radiate from behind them. Then he shook his head, let go of my shirt, and, as I dropped to the floor, his voice changed to a lighter tone. "Oh, and I'm rooting for you to be successful tonight because I actually like you. Should you complete this mission, the head of the CBB has given me permission to shower you handsomely with expensive toys and promote you to be my successor in training. Good luck."

Then Agent Harper bolted out of the room and let the door slam on the way out. I heard his car's engine fire to life, followed by the crunch of gravel as he left, and then I broke down and sobbed right there on the cabin floor.

What the hell was I going to do? How could I get Ava out of this?

I panicked for almost ten minutes before I told myself I had to get up, be a man, and figure out a plausible way to save Ava's life. Harper had bugged the ticket booths, my cabin, my car, and even Ava's boat. I'd be tailed to work and watched carefully. There was no way I could alert Ava to any of this.

I finally drove downtown to the Dairy Queen booth, pretending I had business there. I had one thought, a shot in the dark that might be able to get Ava out of this mess, so I made a quick stop on the way to work to meet with my only chance to save us.

When I arrived at the docks I felt the most horrible feeling. For the first time in my life I dreaded seeing Ava. She came up to visit me after her first trip of the day. I searched her sweet face. There was no way she could be intentionally keeping a dangerous space orb in her house.

Ava took one look at me and knew something was wrong. "Hey, honey, are you okay?" She came close to me and then put her hands around my waist.

Be careful. Don't alarm her.

I kissed her forehead quickly and then pulled away. I couldn't look at her. I couldn't bring myself to smell the coconut scent in her hair when it could be the last time I ever did so.

I tried to act normally so Harper wouldn't know I was up to something. "When are you off tonight?" I asked Ava, but my voice came out all wrong.

Oh, God, I wish I could tell her.

While her shaky voice told me she had the early shift today, she grabbed my hand with a hard squeeze. I could see she was in pain, and it was killing me.

Maybe I could whisper. I could tell her to sneak out of work and go somewhere, anywhere. I slowly moved in for a hug and whispered in her ear, but as I did, a semi blew by the booth, its large engine covering up my whisper. A middle-aged couple with some loud kids walked up to the booth, so I quickly pulled away from Ava.

Dammit!

When the family left I tried another tactic. "Can you come over to the cabin when you are done with work? I've got...something planned." I tried to give her a reassuring smile, but I could tell she was not buying it. I was seeing the pain grow in her face. It was agonizing that I couldn't comfort her at that moment. Then I kissed her forehead again and went back to fake work selling tickets.

The day was absolute hell. I spent the entire shift in a haze trying to orchestrate ways to get us out of the mess. Every time Ava came up to see me, I felt more and more sick, but luckily for me, perhaps, I was swamped with customers, and we didn't get to talk much at all. I suspected the unending crowds were somehow a stunt planned by Harper.

My shift ended when Ava was out on her last tour with Jack. I grabbed a handful of twenties and then threw all the rest of the money and ticket stubs in a drawer under the counter. This was definitely my last day at the boats and perhaps my last day alive, but in case we did escape, we might need a few bucks to get by on before we could establish ourselves somewhere.

I sprinted out to my Audi in the small parking lot near Lower Two. There were no suits that I could see, but when I pulled out of the lot I noticed a dark black Audi with tinted windows pull out after me.

Crap!

I punched the accelerator and heard the engine roar in response. I tried to lose them on the way home, but they had been trained the same way I had been. There was no getting around them.

Brakes screeching, my car slid into the spot in front of my cabin, sending gravel flying everywhere. I flew out of the car and rushed through the cabin door. Locking it behind me, I wedged a chair under the doorknob while I madly gathered a few essentials we could take with us. We needed to get the hell out of Wisconsin as fast as we could. I would deal with her genetic disorder later.

BOOM!

An oversized fist came crashing through the window on the back wall of the cabin and scared the crap out of me. Half a second later, a small army green item came crashing through the window.

Dammit!

They were going to gas me out. Judging by the size of the room, it would only take about thirty seconds. I kicked the chair away from the knob, but right when I opened the front door I felt a bloody fist meet my eye. I hit the floor just as I blacked out.

*   *   *   *

In what felt like seconds later, I came to in a small, very dark, cold room. Agent Harper was sitting on a chair under a naked light bulb hanging from a silver chain in the ceiling. I had been placed on a chair too, but my hands were tied behind my back with rope. A laptop was sitting open on a small circular table in front of me. Its screen was black.

"Nolan..." He growled like a small, ugly dog. "I warned you not to alert the Carrier!" He did not sound happy, like every bit of good was squeezed out of him.

"I didn't tell her anything!" I protested. Something about the situation did not feel right. And then it dawned on me. How did I not see it before? I am such an idiot. "I don't work for a covert branch of the FBI, do I?" I had been knocked out and then tied to a chair by my boss. This was all too nefarious for the FBI.

Harper released a truly evil laugh. "Oh, Agent Hill." There was a pause as he stood up from the chair. How could I have ever thought that face was kind? Maybe it was the bad lighting, but Harper looked downright wicked now. "No. You do not work for the FBI. You never have. Although the CBB's mission is to keep the American people safe at all costs, the government won't condone our methods, pronouncing them unethical and corrupt."

I couldn't believe it! How could I have been working for the CBB and not know it wasn't part of the

FBI? I could feel the anger rising inside of me. I had been betrayed and used.

He walked behind me, continuing to lecture. "Ten years ago when the CBB was rejected by the government, Ethan Myers, a founding member, broke away and secretly formed his own covert operations. He hired Americans as field agents and made them believe they were working for a legitimate government function."

"You son of a bit..." but I was cut off by a deeper and more urgent voice emerging from the shadows.

"Now, now, Agent Hill. Save your curse words for when I'm absent." The man's voice was steady and confident. "I know you've just been blindsided by the truth, but I suggest you think logically about this. The CBB has provided well for you these past three years. You can't deny that." He walked into the light, and I could see his face clearly for the first time.

"Ethan Myers." It came out as a surprised whisper. I would recognize his face anywhere. The field agents at the CBB had been trained to recognize Myers as an enemy of the US government. We believed he was involved in treason, espionage, and designing genetic weapons. And now he was standing right before me.

A large bead of sweat began to drip down the side of my face. We must have been trained to know him as an enemy so we would further believe we were working for the FBI. Or perhaps there was another agenda I just couldn't figure out in my mind right now. I was so angry I had been deceived in this way. I had sacrificed a real life in order to fight for good—but not for whatever this was.

"Let me make something clear, Agent Hill. The Carrier and the space rock need to be destroyed within the next three hours. And you are the only one to do it." Myers sat down in the chair at the other side of the table and casually crossed one leg over the other.

"That's bullshit. Any one of your monkeys could take her out!"

What was I saying?

I wanted to take it back the second it came out of my mouth. I struggled with the ropes behind my back angrily, and wiggled in my chair, frustrated.

Harper and Myers laughed as they watched me realize what a fool I was. Myers nodded at Harper, and he walked over to the computer sitting on the table. "Maybe this will persuade you." He turned it on and played the video waiting on the screen. It was my mother, father, and sister tied to chairs and looking like they had been drugged. My mother was moaning, and I saw blood dripping from my father's hairline. My sister sat lifeless.

I bit my bottom lip and tasted blood in my mouth. They wanted me to become agitated, weak. But the video could be completely fabricated for all I knew. I tried to hide my solicitude, so I looked Ethan Myers directly in the eyes and said nothing.

"Fine. If that's the way you want it." Myers stood up from his chair. "You've made your decision. I'll send my field agents to take care of Miss Gardner immediately, and then I have no use for you or your family."

And then I remembered the plan I had hatched that morning. A plan that had only the slightest chance of succeeding, but could possibly save the ones I loved.

Myers gave a nod to one of the suits standing near the door. Then Myers and Agent Harper turned to leave just as the bodyguard grabbed me from behind with a burly arm across my chest. Then he brandished a knife in front of my face and brought it slowly to my neck. It was now or never.

"WAIT! Wait! I'll do it!" The man lowered his knife but held his hold across my chest. Harper and Myers stopped dead in their tracks. Myers turned around wearing a disturbing smile. Then in a voice that was barely there, I said, "I'll do it."

Myers walked right over to me, put his hand on my shoulder and whispered in my ear, "That's a good boy, Agent Hill." His voice was like poison in my ear, and his smell was disgusting. He let a hand run over my hair a few times like I was his pet dog. I growled a little under my breath as Myers pulled away from me. Harper whispered something to the bodyguard, and then he and Myers left the room.

The door to the little room slammed shut and the guard took several slow steps towards me, smiling nefariously. "Boss said to let you go, but how would that be any fun?"

This was trouble.

I shoved my thumb in the heart of the knot behind my back and had the rope untied by the time the guard reached me. I ducked just as the guard swung his fist and then I leapt up on the seat of the chair and tipped the backrest down with my left foot. I caught him by surprise and in a split second I whipped up the chair by the back and swung it—CRACK!—right across the bodyguard's head. He fell to the floor like a sack of potatoes with a loud thud.

I took a second to catch my breath, and then I felt his pulse. He was gone. I picked up his knife and ran out of there as fast as I could, trying not to think about my first kill.

When I busted through the heavy steel door, the light of late afternoon burned my eyes. I squinted around. I was at some type of warehouse in the middle of nowhere. They had driven my Audi there and parked it outside the door, apparently for when I agreed to go kill Ava. How nice of them. I hopped in and turned on my dashboard GPS. It indicated I was outside of town about two miles from the cabin.

I drove as fast as I could all the way back and called no one as I drove—the car was surely bugged. They had seen and heard it all. All summer we had been watched. I couldn't believe it. It was all my fault. I had led them to Ava, and now they expected me to kill her or they would do us both in along with my entire family.

I flew into the alley behind Animal Island. Ava's car was there and my heart stopped momentarily. *Dammit*! Had they sent someone to take care of Ava?

I screeched the tires to a halt within inches of my cabin's front steps. I left the driver's side door open as I carefully inched my way to the front door. I pressed my ear to the door listening for noises inside, but heard nothing.

A small, wailing sound led me around the back of the cabin. Wishing I had been issued a gun, I carefully peaked around the sidewall into the back yard. Ava was crumpled into a ball on the grass, crying hysterically.

Oh my God.

I ran to her. "Ava! Are you hurt?"

What did they do to her?

I knelt down on the grass beside her and slid my arms around her waist. She settled right into my body and held on tight. I let out a breath of relief. She was okay...for now. Her wonderful smells flooded my heart with a million emotions. She sat up and looked at me through her tears.

"Please, sweet Ava, tell me what's wrong. Are you hurt?" I couldn't hold back my own tears as I held her sweet face in my hands. Was this the last time I'd be able to sense her heart beating with mine? I kissed her with everything I had, and she kissed me back.

I knew we were being watched and time was running out. I quickly picked her up and carried her to the front seat of my car. Then I got in and peeled away from Animal Island. My body was shaking with fear and anger and my mind was flooded with a million thoughts as I sped down Minnesota Avenue.

Judging by the level of the sun beneath the trees, it was pretty close to sunset. Myers's field agents had most likely raided the Gardner house by now and were apprehending Ava's parents as we spoke. I prayed to God they didn't hurt her mom and dad.

I parked and shut off the ignition, but stayed in the car staring silently out the windshield, tears streaming down my face. I didn't know if I could go through with it. I knew that once today was done, I could never see Ava again.

I didn't want the summer to end. I didn't want our relationship to end. I was beyond frustrated at this point. Ava reached for my hand, but I pulled it away. If she only knew what I was about to do.

Time was running out, but I was losing my nerve. I dropped my head into my hands and said a quick prayer. With my whole body shaking, I slammed my fist into the steering wheel and scared Ava half to death. Then I lifted my head and screamed in anger at the ceiling of the car. I was sure Harper and Myers were wearing earpieces, and I hoped I just blew their eardrums out.

I looked down at the clock on the dashboard—8:46.

Now. It's time.

I leaned over and told Ava in a whispered voice to say nothing. I didn't want the bugs picking up any clues to where we were going. Then I opened the door and waited impatiently for her to come around the front of the car. In one swift motion I grabbed her hand tightly and set off running toward Make Out Rock. I heard a train honking its horn down the tracks several hundred yards away. We jumped over the train tracks and ran through the bushes. We descended down the deep path until we were at the rock cliff.

I trembled as I grabbed her by the shoulders and looked her straight in the eye. She was more beautiful now than ever before. My heart was breaking over and over again as she looked at me with fear in her eyes. The train was speeding behind us so loudly I had to yell to her that we didn't have much time.

She was screaming back at me, more confused than ever. I wished I could explain, but there was no time. Then she yelled, "Nolan, I love you. You can tell me anything!"

She loves me? Why did she have to say that?

My voice was caught in the back of my throat, but I was able to choke out, "I love you, too." Then I kissed her like we were back in the cave on the Upper Dells again. It was filled with raw emotion. She held onto me tightly. If we could stay on this rock forever kissing...but I knew it was now or never. The train had almost passed.

I found the smallest amount of courage I had left inside of me, looked into her eyes, and whimpered, "I'm so sorry it has to be this way. I truly do love you, Ava Gardner." And then I pulled the knife from my belt and, with all the force I could muster up, I shoved it deep into her torso with a grunt. I kissed her one last time on the forehead while I hysterically sobbed into her hair.

Then I threw the knife down on the rock with disgust, and, without looking back, I ran up the path. The caboose of the train had just barely passed as I crossed the tracks and retched into the darkness on the other side of the pathway. My head began to pound as I willed myself to stand and stumble back to my car. The grass was spinning, and I couldn't tell which way was up.

When I finally arrived back to my car, Harper was there waiting. I swung at his face, but my body had nothing left in it and my dizzy brain caused me to miss horribly. The momentum of the punch spun me around in a circle and I came to rest bracing myself on the hood of the car with my hands. I stood up, leaving bloody handprints for Harper to see.

Harper laughed maniacally as he swiped a finger in Ava's red blood. He pressed his finger to a small black machine in his hand. It beeped after a few seconds and a robotic voice announced that the sample contained extremely elevated counts of radiation.

"Well, well, Agent Hill. I have to say, I am impressed. First you escaped my man back at the factory, and now you actually had the guts to kill the Carrier. Ethan had little faith in you, but I was sure you'd go through with it. Now, there is no time to waste. You must join me in preventing a little blue rock from blowing the Midwest off the map."

Sick, breathing heavily, and full of rage, I turned toward Agent Harper. "You and the CBB can rot in hell." I was banking on the hope that Harper wouldn't find Ava back through the trees for a while, and I had no idea what was going to happen to me next, but I didn't care.

Without displaying any emotion, he said, "Agent Hill, you disappoint me. Oh well, that's too bad. I guess Myers was right—the CBB has no use for you."

Then I heard a loud bang and instantly my world went black.

Epilogue

The hospital bed was too hard and the fluorescent lights were too harsh. I kept my eyes closed as I tried to figure out where I was. I was very uncomfortable and quite disorientated. The pain in my side was too much as I tried to sit up. Then I heard a soft voice from the bedside.

"Don't try to move just yet. You've had a few operations but you are safe now." It was a female voice I didn't recognize.

"Nolan?" I managed to squeak out. The voice said nothing but gently applied a cold washcloth to my forehead.

"Don't talk now. Just relax."

I shut my eyes and slept—not because I wanted to, but because I couldn't help it. I dreamt of flying over the beautiful brown river, gracefully darting around the Lower Dells. I flew next to the cliffs and then swooped down close to the river, skimming it with my hand. I examined my body in the reflection of the water and expected to see a bird, but there were no feathers, and I had no wings. I was perfectly human.

Flying felt absolutely wonderful and free—I felt truly happy. But then I looked back into the water and saw the reflection of a dark cloud roll in above my head. Flying right above me was a scary, hooded figure holding a sharp, shiny knife. The hood was slowly removed, and I saw Nolan's face staring at me with a menacing grin.

I woke up with a loud gasp. I sat up quickly in bed, sweating and breathing heavily. My hand instinctively went to the place at my side where I had felt hot, radiating pain. There was a nurse in the room checking the machines by my bed and she rushed over.

"Where are my parents?" I asked the nurse.

"No one can see you right now. Try to rest." She helped me lie back down. I felt a distant pain in the back of my head, but was able to fall asleep relatively quickly.

It was only a few hours later, I thought, when I woke up and saw my mother by my bedside. She looked like she hadn't slept in days.

"Mom? Oh thank God! What happened? Where's Dad?"

"Oh sweetheart, your father is gone on a work trip. He wants me to tell you he's thinking about you and feeling horrible that he can't be here by your bedside right now."

I smiled for my mother. Fear struck my heart as my mind changed thoughts. There was something else weighing on my mind. "Did they catch Nolan?" I asked my mother. "Is he in jail?" My heart ached a little at my words.

"No, sweetie. Actually, he's lying in a hospital bed down the hallway." Her eyes looked bloodshot like she had been crying.

"He's hurt, too?" My heart perked up, wondering what could have happened after I was stabbed. "What happened after he left me?" My mom was reluctant to say anything. "Oh, Mom. Would you please tell me what happened last night?"

My mother grabbed my hand gently and took her time saying, "The doctors don't think your body is ready to handle the truth of what happened that night. They think you might go into shock."

"Mom. I loved him. I think I need to know the truth in order to heal." I looked at her with imploring eyes. My mother's were beginning to tear up. She put a soft hand on my arm.

"He loved you, too, Ava. He and I had a heart-to-heart this morning. He is quite a special man." She patted me on the knees and I wondered what had been said in that conversation.

I took a really good look at my mother. She had large bags under her eyes, and her skin color looked a little off. Her hair somehow seemed thinner and she looked weak. What had happened to her? She looked like hell.

My eyes began to fill with tears. All I wanted was to ask Nolan a million questions.

"Go to sleep now, Ava. When you are well enough, I promise you'll get all your questions answered."

* * * *

My mother's voice woke me gently from my sleep. "Ava honey, you have a visitor."

Nolan?

I opened my eyes and anxiously looked toward the door.

"Hey, hot stuff! You're looking great!"

"Ted." A smile fell across my face. "It is so good to see you."

He sat down on the chair by my bed. My mother very graciously excused herself to the waiting room and closed the door gently as she exited.

Ted's expression turned somber. "You know, I thought you weren't going to make it there for a while."

"Ted. What the hell happened last night? I thought for sure I was going to die." I knew he'd tell me the truth even if the doctors thought I couldn't handle it.

Ted looked confused for a second. "Last night? Oh, honey, no one told you?"

"Told me what?" I didn't like how this was going.

"Well...you've been here in the hospital for almost two weeks."

"What?" I couldn't believe my ears. How could I have been here for so long? "After Nolan"—it was hard to say it out loud—"stabbed me...how did I get off the rock?"

"I don't know all the details, but I'll tell you what I do know. First of all, Nolan is an FBI agent. Or at least he thought he was."

"Funny, Ted. Now quit trying to cheer me up." He said nothing for a moment and when I looked into his eyes, I saw he was telling the truth.

"What? There's no way!" I had spent almost the whole summer with him and felt like I knew him better than I knew myself. How could I not have known that he worked for a federal agency? But then I remembered the briefcase of gadgets I found under his bed before the Fourth of July party.

Ted went on. "He was placed in the Dells as a field agent this summer." Then that friendly Ted-smile that I had come to love made an appearance. "I knew there was something fishy about that dude."

I laughed nervously at his comment. Something fishy, indeed.

"Anyway—and here's where I'm a little shaky on the details—there is something about you and your family that the authorities were investigating."

"What? Me and my family?"

"Yeah, something about that blue rock in your bedroom. So anyway, Nolan's boss thought you and your family were going to use the rock to create some sort of nuclear weapon and decided that you needed to die for your criminal plots. Oh, and he also decided that Nolan was the one who was supposed to kill you."

"That rock is nuclear? The FBI will kill you if you are a criminal? I'm so confused!"

"Now Ava, try to pay attention. I said Nolan *thought* he worked for the FBI. Turned out it was some evil man named Myers who headed up some covert, fake government outfit and made Nolan believe he worked for the FBI." He took a big breath. "Anyway, Nolan had no choice but to pray you didn't die and hope I would find you in time."

"Wait, wait, wait. *You* came to rescue me?" I was shocked. I didn't know Ted and Nolan had any communications since that night at the Dairy Queen booth. "You've gotta back up. I had no idea you two were friends."

"Well, not friends, exactly, but Nolan understood the friendship you and I share. He knew if you were in trouble, I wouldn't think twice about coming to help you out."

I was trying to put it all together in my brain, but it still wasn't making sense. My face must have displayed my confusion because Ted went on.

"The morning of the night you were stabbed, Nolan showed up downtown when I was driving shuttle. He pulled me around the corner to the alleyway and spoke in whispers. I could tell there was something wrong, so I paid careful attention even though I never trusted the guy. Nolan gave me a black box with a screen on the top and told me that I needed to watch it all day. It was a GPS device, and if the light on the top lit up, it meant that I needed to follow the directions on the screen to find the other tracking piece. He said you might be in trouble, and I was the only one who could save you from serious danger. I had no clue what he meant, but he looked so stressed and serious that I got the feeling I should do what he said. Before I could ask him any questions, he told me you would thank me later and then left quickly. I immediately called you, but you must've had your phone turned off on the boat."

I listened, not knowing exactly what it all could mean.

"I kept that box on me all day, and it did absolutely nothing. I tried calling your phone several times, but you never answered. Then after work, I was trying to distract myself by watching TV with Mr. Kitty when the thing lit up like a Christmas tree. The screen showed a map of the area by the community pool, and there was a little star labeled 'Ava' right on top of Make Out Rock. At first I thought it was some kind of little joke or something, but then I thought about Nolan's demeanor downtown that morning, and I figured I needed to check it out.

"I drove my butt down to the rock as fast as I could and ran all the way down the tracks to the rock. That's when I about crapped my pants. You were lying there unconscious in a pool of blood, and sitting on top of your shoulder was a tiny black button sticker emitting the same lights as the ones on top of the GPS box in my hand. I called 911 immediately, and they rushed you off to this hospital. You went through surgery to repair the kidney that he barely brushed with the knife."

My jaw was stuck in the open position. This all seemed farfetched, but I didn't think Ted could make up something like that. "That clears things up a bit, although I still have a lot of questions," I said. "One of which being, if I had surgery that night, then why have I been in the hospital for two weeks? And where am I exactly? Some kind of high-tech hospital?"

"I'm not sure I'm the best person to answer all those questions. It gets pretty technical from here, but it has something to do with that blue rock at your house. Apparently it's been emitting some type of crazy space radiation and you and your family had to go through some kind of futuristic gene therapy here at the Milwaukee FBI hospital or you'd turn into psychos."

A laugh snuck out of my lips. "Ah, Ted, I'm pretty sure you made that up." I shook my head with disbelief.

"Not even one word. Absolutely not." He looked very seriously at me.

"So that's why my mom looks sick?" I suddenly felt a chill and pulled the thin hospital blanket up to my chin.

"Yes. Apparently the rest of your family got the least of the radiation, but they were all treated."

"It was in my room," I whispered quietly and Ted went on.

"You had much higher levels of radiation and had to undergo pretty intense therapy, but the FBI doctors believe you all will be completely normal."

"Wow... Okay, that is a lot to take in." I stared at the wall for a moment thinking about everything Ted had just told me. Then I reached over and squeezed his hand. "Thank you, Ted, for saving my life." I smiled at him, and he mirrored my face back to me.

"Not at all, my dear."

I had a lot more questions for Ted, but my doctor came in and decided it was time for him to leave and let me get some rest. Ted said he'd be back to see me the next day.

That night I was feeling much better and decided I couldn't wait any longer to see Nolan. As soon as the night nurse believed I had fallen asleep, I carefully got out of bed and shuffled over to the door. I stuck my head out and looked down to the nurse's station. It was very quiet and there wasn't any movement in the hallway, so I crept out of the door and walked down the hallway until I saw Nolan's name on a doorplate.

My heart stopped for what felt like many seconds. I looked back at the nurse's station. No movement. With shaking hands, I slowly pushed open the door to Nolan's room. My heart dropped into my stomach when I saw him lying there on the bed. His blue eyes were closed, and he looked so peaceful. Although I could tell he had been sick, he still was breathtakingly beautiful to me.

My brain flashed back to the moment he stabbed me and I panicked. I quickly backtracked toward to door to leave, but then I heard him speak.

"Ava?" His voice was hoarse like he hadn't used it in many days. "My beautiful Ava?"

I said nothing as I took a step back towards him. The corners of his mouth turned up ever so slightly.

"Can't stay away, huh?" He stared at me with those baby blue eyes, and I could feel my heart melting. "I am so ecstatic you are alive." Then he restated. "Actually, I was pretty darned sure I would miss all your major organs." He chuckled a little under his breath, but then grimaced with pain. He paused and searched my face. He raised his hand slowly off the bed and motioned for me to take the chair next to him. "Could you ever find it within yourself to forgive me?"

I didn't know what to say. There were so many questions still in my mind. If what Ted said was true, then Nolan was a good guy. But how could he be good if he had lied to me for the past three months?

I began with the most basic question. "Nolan Hill, who are you?"

He smiled and took my hand. "I guess I owe you that much." Then he looked deep into my eyes and very slowly said, "My name is Nolan Hill. I am a twenty-four-year-old native of Chicago, and I am in desperate, all-encompassing love with you, Ava Gardner."

And for now, that was all I needed to hear. I leaned over and kissed him sweetly, hoping he could feel forgiveness in my lips.

Acknowledgments

My deepest gratitude to my husband, Wes, who although he may have wanted to, he never once rolled his eyes, scoffed, or openly reprimanded me whenever I (yet again) cracked open my laptop to dive into my world of Ava and Nolan (especially when I should have been cleaning the house, doing the laundry, or making dinner instead). Thank you so much for allowing me to chase my dreams. I love you!

Many thanks to my personal cheerleaders, Mindy and Lori, who had the loudest voices in raising me up into a level of confidence that could bring me to this accomplishment. I couldn't have reached this point without you!

To my benevolent editor, Carl Stratman, who offered me phenomenal suggestions, careful edits, and a cheap service! Without your generosity, I don't think this would have been possible.

A big thank you to my awesome graphic designer, Hannah Christian Hess, whose creative efforts blew my mind! Thank you so much for your willingness to help me out! www.hannahchristian.com

Thanks to all the readers who gave my debut novel a try! I hope you'll stay tuned for the next installment of The Carrier Series!

And finally, with grateful appreciation deep in my heart, thank you, Lena, for your positive support, your willingness to research for me, and your truthful advice. Love you.

Excerpt from the next book in The Carrier Series:
The Defender

Nolan parked his silver Audi near the baseball fields behind the community pool. He pushed the button on the dash to turn off the engine, and then reached over to grab my hand. My insides felt like there were a thousand tiny daggers poking my organs. I squeezed Nolan's hand for comfort. It was his idea to visit the place where our lives drastically changed a bit more than six weeks before, but I wasn't sure if I was ready just yet.

Nolan let out a deep sigh. "Are you ready for this?"

I closed my eyes and took a deep breath, trying to suppress the horror of that night, but I couldn't keep the thoughts from my brain. I was stabbed and left to die right on that rock in the distance. But I knew Nolan was right—visiting Make Out Rock was part of our healing.

Nolan narrowed his eyes with concern and then placed his other hand on top of our already interlaced fingers.

I smiled weakly. How does he always make me feel so safe?

"Yes. Ready or not, let's do this." Then I let go of his hand and reached for the door handle. I rubbed my stomach—the daggers were still poking.

Was this really a great idea?

Nolan met me around the front bumper with his arms open wide. I walked right into them and they closed around me like safety gates. I snuggled the side of my head into the crook under his shoulder. It was my favorite spot to be.

Nolan lowered his face into my hair, inhaled deeply, and loudly exhaled. I knew he was smelling my hair—a habit of his that I treasured. "Let's go over there before I chicken out," he said.

Ah ha. So he felt a little nervous as well.

Nolan let go of my back, grabbed my shoulders, and held me at arms length. "Ava Gardner, you are the reason for my existence. I swear to heaven above that I will do everything in my power to keep you safe from evil."

I giggled a little. "Safe from evil? Sounds like a comic book line."

"You'd be surprised how much this life resembles the world of comic books." He gently kissed my lips, making my knees wonderfully weak, and then grabbed my left hand and led me off in the direction of the train tracks.

Today the sky was a brilliant blue backdrop to the fluffy white clouds. A gentle breeze with a tiny bite of cold Wisconsin air blew the hair from my sweater-covered shoulders. It was a beautiful fall day by anyone's standards. The tree's leaves were just beginning to display their gorgeous colors, and I could faintly hear a tour boat chugging its way down the Wisconsin River off in the distance.

As we crossed the train tracks, I could feel Nolan's hand begin to shake in mine. He was the one who stabbed me, but it was a warranted part of a desperate plan to save my life from a sinister man who thought I was a hardened criminal. Messed up? Yes, I knew. But even so, last summer was a chapter of my life that I wouldn't change for anything. It was one that helped me find the love of my life. I wanted nothing more than to be with Nolan Hill for the rest of my days and I was pretty sure he felt the exact same way.

The thick, green screen of trees and bushes that hid the entrance to Make Out Rock in the summer was now lying in heaps of red and yellow leaves at the foot of bare branches, leaving the entrance exposed and open. We easily found the deep-cut pathway and scaled our way down to the top of the towering rock ledge.

Partway down I stopped dead in my tracks as my mind quickly flashed back to that dark night. Nolan felt me drawback, and stopped his momentum to wrap his arms around my body. My knees began to shake and my stomach turned over, but at the same time I knew this was a mental hurdle I'd have to jump.

Nolan began to rub the side of my arms and kissed my forehead sweetly. "Maybe I was wrong. Let's get out of here. We can visit in a few months."

I looked up through the tears forming in my eyes. How was I lucky enough to love someone who loved me even more in return? I wanted him to understand. "No, Nolan. I want to do this." I looked down at the ground, gravity pulling a tiny tear out of my eye. "Although that was the worst night of my life, I need to be here with you now. To prove to myself that I can move on." The daggers were still dancing in my stomach.

Nolan's blue eyes glittered in the autumn sunlight. He placed his fingers on my jawline, stroking my chin with his thumb. I felt like melting right into his hand. He opened his mouth to speak a few times but said nothing.

Finally he said, "I would feel humbled and gracious if you could find it within yourself to someday forgive me and trust me once more. I know it will take time, but I am willing to wait as long as it takes."

Then before I could answer, he slowly pulled me in and held his lips half an inch from mine. His warm breath lingered on my mouth and wanted so much for him to go the rest of the distance, but he held his position, teasing me carefully. Right as I was ready to go in for the touchdown myself, he sensed my impatience, and kissed me with much emotion.

I led Nolan by the hand to the middle of the rock ledge, and we both sat down. The familiar beauty of the Dells had calmed my breathing, and I could feel the daggers backing off. A deep, cleansing breath of the natural air refreshed my lungs. I watched the gentle, swirling brown water flow down river and my mind was flooded with memories of a summer filled with adventures with Nolan. Falling in love with him had been easy and natural.

Nolan looked upriver toward the docks. "I realized that night that you were the most important person in my life. I knew I needed to do whatever I could in order to protect you, even if that meant harming you in the process."

Did he know I felt the same way?

"That day," I began, "when I knew something was wrong and I was sure you were going to break up with me, I literally felt like my life was over. I had been through heartbreak before, but nothing compared to the pain I went through that night. That's when I knew, I had given you my heart."

I leaned my head onto his shoulder and we continued to look around, taking in the beauty of the environment around us. I looked down toward the end of the rock ledge and couldn't help but imagine the exact position I was in when I lay here waiting for death to take me away that night. Then I noticed a dark stain on the rock where I had lain.

My blood.

Of course, my blood had stained the rock. All of a sudden I flashed back to that moment when I truly thought my life had ended. When someone I loved and trusted purposely shoved a knife into my belly.

I stood up, shaking. "Let's get going. I think I've had enough for one day."

"Absolutely." He rose and turned to leave. "Are you alri—" But then he stopped abruptly, made a weird face, and scanned the area around us.

"What's wrong?" He put two fingers over my lips to silence me.

He whispered, "Shh...listen," as his ears turned up like a Lab on a hunt.

I heard it, too. A very faint beeping noise. Its high-pitched warning tone was rapidly getting faster and faster.

"Run!" he screamed, and pulled my arm toward the railroad tracks. I begged my feet to go faster but I couldn't seem to make them keep up with Nolan's. A wild scream escaped my lips as he leaped over the tracks and dove into the ditch behind them. I followed his lead and right as I landed, Nolan rolled over my body and an ear splitting BOOM echoed out over the river and through the baseball fields. My hands instinctively covered my ears and I screamed again.

Nolan waited a few seconds and then rolled off of me. We sat up on our elbows and looked toward the rock. The whole cliff top had been blown away. Thick, angry smoke took over the air, and fire began to eat the bottom of the trees. My jaw was stuck in the open position.

My Dells! My beautiful Dells blown away!

Nolan stood up. "Are you okay?"

My ears were ringing but I could still hear Nolan. I took a quick inventory of the rest of my body, running my hands up and down my legs, torso, and arms. All parts were accounted for and I could see no blood. "Yeah. I think I'm fine." My head stayed focused on the scene before me.

"We have to get out of here!" Nolan held out his hand to help me up, but I was still in awe of what had happened. Why was he in such a hurry to leave?

I couldn't take my eyes off the scene at hand. "We have to call 911."

Nolan began yelling, "They won't be far away! We have to go *now*!"

"Who won't be far away?"

Nolan yanked me onto my feet and pulled me in the opposite direction of his car, toward a grassy pathway parallel with the train tracks. I kept looking over my shoulder, causing my body to twist and my legs to flail, not being able to keep up with my top half.

Nolan stopped and grabbed my face in his hands. He looked deep into my eyes and said with great authority, "Ava Gardner. You have to trust me. We need to run down this path as fast as we can. *Now*!"

I stared with disbelief. Was I dreaming? It wasn't until I heard the police sirens behind us that I snapped out of my trance and began to run.

Nolan led the way, sprinting through the forest. My heart was beating out of my chest, and I didn't think I could go much farther. We must have been running at full speed for at least five minutes. I was not used to such nonsense.

Finally he stopped and surveyed the scene. "This will do," he said.

I bent over with my hands on my knees, breathing like I had just given birth right there on the forest floor. He told me to climb halfway up the tree and sit on a sturdy limb.

"No!...Not until...you tell me...what's going...on!" I could barely get the words out between my heavy breathing. I was beyond frustration.

Nolan quickly walked over to me. He pulled me up from my crouched position and stared deeply into my eyes. "My sweet Ava. Please. I know this must be hard, but you have to trust me. Do as I say and this will all be over in a few minutes." Then he kissed me passionately but quickly. "Please."

I wanted to protest but instead I surrendered to those damn baby blues. I was helpless against their power.

I turned around and climbed the tree up to the third limb. I was lucky my sister and I had trees to climb in our backyard as kids. Who knew that skill would come in handy as an adult? I looked down. I was probably about forty feet up the tree and glad that heights didn't bother me.

Nolan nervously paced the forest floor under my hideout tree. He took out his cell and dialed a number. Then he turned his back away from me. Normally I would be able to hear what he was saying, but my ears were still ringing from the blast. My stomach had turned inside out again. I was nervous and anxious and sure of one thing—I would *never* go near that rock again.

I could see the smoke rising from the site a few hundred yards down the pathway. There was a fire truck there now with men pointing long hoses at the fire.

Nolan's voice grew louder. "Dammit! I need a reconnaissance team in here now!" He began to pace quicker. "What do you mean my field rating is unsatisfactory?" He paused and I could tell he was angry. "A civilian's life is at risk!"

Nolan suddenly slammed a finger at the screen to hang up the call, letting out a grunt of frustration in the process. He quickly and intensely looked up over the tree line. Had he heard something I didn't? Then out of nowhere the crack of gunshot echoed through the woods and Nolan dropped to the ground with a groan.

I gasped. *No...no...no...no!* My mouth opened to let out a scream but nothing came out.

Nolan rolled over to his side, looked up at me, and said in a raspy voice, "Greeeeeeeeen. Trust Greene."

I whispered back through my tears, "What? Sweetheart...?"

I was about to jump down from the tree when I heard footsteps. I looked out into the forest and saw three men in dark suits carrying guns. They ran towards the unmoving Nolan. I held completely still. They hadn't seen me up in the tree yet.

One of the men pressed something in his ear, "We got him. No sign of the girl."

They knew I had been with Nolan. Chills sped down my spine. Another man picked up Nolan and threw him over his shoulder, and then they all ran out of the forest the same way they entered.

Uncontrollable tears began to fall from my eyes. What just happened? This couldn't be real! A nightmare, this had to be a nightmare.

Wake up, Ava!

I slapped myself in the face, but lost my balance on the tree limb and fell backwards, narrowly missing all the branches on the way down. My body landed with a thud on the grass and weeds below, and I let out a groan as I rolled to my left. My right arm radiated intense pain.

Oh no! I probably broke it.

I knew I had to get out of there before someone else came. But should I run after Nolan's captors or toward my parents' house? I wasn't prepared for any kind of fight so I painfully set off in the direction of Capital Street. I scrambled about four steps forward before I heard a loud crack and felt a sting in my back, sending me instantly to the ground.

I'd been shot, too. What kind of evil world would bring us together only to rip us apart time and time again?

Well, at least I could join Nolan in heaven.

Diana Ryan lives in the great state of Wisconsin with her husband and two young children. Although writing was not her first career, publishing a novel has always been on her bucket list. In her free time, she enjoys watching live theater, playing piano, hanging out with her family, and of course, writing sequels to Ava and Nolan's adventures.

55893019R00142

Made in the USA
Lexington, KY
06 October 2016